Giant Killers

GW00731776

The stories so far. Other books in the Team Mates series (in order):

Giant Killers

Paul Cockburn

Virgin

Thanks to Elaine for the advice.

First published in Great Britain in 1996 by
Virgin Books
an imprint of Virgin Publishing Ltd
332 Ladbroke Grove
London W10 5AH

Copyright © Paul Cockburn 1996

The right of Paul Cockburn to be identified as the author
of this work has been asserted by him in accordance
with the Copyright Designs and Patents Act 1988.

This book is sold subject to the condition that it shall not,
by way of trade or otherwise, be lent, resold, hired out or
otherwise circulated without the publisher's prior written
consent in any form of binding or cover other than that
in which it is published and without a similar condition
including this condition being imposed upon the
subsequent purchaser.

A catalogue record for this book is available from the
British Library.

ISBN 0 7535 0051 5

Typeset by Galleon Typesetting, Ipswich
Printed and bound by
BPC Paperbacks Ltd, Aylesbury

*To my father. He had a trial
for Fulham in the thirties y'know . . .
Now look at them . . .*

One

—⚽—

'I've got you now, Billy Murdoch,' the boy called through the open doorway. 'Hiding in there isn't going to save you for long. You have to come out in the end.'

There was no answer.

'I reckon as you'll be getting right cold,' the boy continued. He listened carefully for any movement. The wind stirred fitfully, chilling and bitter when it touched bare skin. He was feeling fairly uncomfortable himself, even wearing a long top coat. He knew Billy had nothing more than a ragged pullover, with more holes than wool, plus a flimsy shirt and a pair of shorts. He must be freezing . . .

Aye, but he's out of the wind, at least, the boy realised, scowling at the darkened doorway. He took a look around, wondering if he should try to creep in.

The trouble was that at the other end of the long, brick-built out-building, there was a second door. Out here, the large boy could keep both doors in sight, but he knew that if he set foot inside, Billy would be out of the other door like greased lightning. The little thief had led him a merry dance already and there was no way he was going to chase him any further. If only he could barricade one door while he went through the other . . .

He continued to look around the yard, hoping to see something he could use to block off the open doorway. There was nothing. He turned back and listened carefully once more. He could hear water dripping, but nothing to betray at which end of the block Billy Murdoch might be hiding.

Frustration made the boy even more angry. His breath clouded in front of his face as he cursed the target of his temper.

'You'll not get away, Billy Murdoch,' he threatened. 'Not this time.'

All the same, he had no plan that would allow him to get at Billy. It was a stand-off.

'You're just making it worse for yourself!' he raged abruptly, his voice echoing off the buildings around him. He caught himself quickly. The caretaker's house wasn't that far from where he stood and he had seen lights in the windows as he ran up the hill. The last thing he wanted was for anyone to rob him of his prey at this late hour, not after all the trouble he had been to tracking Billy down.

Even as he felt that pang of worry, he heard a voice call from the other side of the yard. The caretaker? The boy slunk back into the shadows at the end of the block, watching nervously as someone came into the yard, skulking over by the gate. Then he realised the newcomer was calling his name.

'Jack! Jack, it's me, Tom!'

'Over here!' the boy hissed, and he stepped back out into the moonlight, feeling lighthearted with relief. Tommy Baxter! Tommy must have followed Jack and Billy as they left the market. Jack had been sure they'd left everyone behind, but dogged old Tom had slogged along in their wake and finally caught them up! Now the tables were turned.

'What are we doing here?' laughed Tom, his face betraying his amazement as he looked around at their location. It had been a while since either of them had been to school.

'The runt's trapped in here,' replied Jack, jerking his finger through the dark doorway.

'Why'd he come here?' asked Tom, who was clearly not concentrating on the matter at hand.

'What does it matter?' Jack cursed. 'He's here. And now we've got him!' He pointed at the other doorway, at the far end of the block. 'You go in there, and I'll –'

'I'm not going in!' protested Tom. 'It's dark – and it stinks!'

Jack sighed in despair, gripping his fists into tight balls. 'Of course it stinks,' he muttered. 'It's a khazi, isn't it? And it hasn't got any lights, so it's bound to be dark, isn't it?'

'I hate this place . . .' moaned Tom, looking along the whole length of the dismal, damp building. 'I never used it when we was at school here . . . I'd always wait until I could go home . . .'

Jack took hold of his mate and shook him. The last thing that could possibly interest him at the moment was a story of Tom's

2

schooldays. Jack remembered White Hill Board School with just the same amount of loathing as his mate, but right now it was just buildings on a quiet winter's night. No teacher was going to come out into the yard to ask what they were doing; there would be no appearance by old Mr Crane, the bald, brutal, beaky headmaster. No, there was just the two of them and Billy Murdoch, and the chance to deal out some of the punishment they had always had to endure.

'Look,' he whispered. 'You don't have to go in, right? Just stand by the far door and make sure he can't escape. I'll go in here, and flush him out . . .'

Tom giggled nervously. 'Flush him out! That's good, that is!'

Jack cuffed him around the ear, making the other boy wail.

'Do as I say! I want Billy Murdoch caught, and I want him right now. Just do your part, will you?'

Tom rubbed his ear, which stood out from his close-cropped head, glowing almost bright pink with the cold. He managed to look quite sorry for himself, but Jack was in no mood to apologise. He grabbed his mate by the coat and turned him round, pushing him towards the other door.

When he was satisfied that Tom was in place, Jack gritted his teeth and took his first step into the building.

Immediately, he was engulfed by the cold blackness, the damp and the unpleasant smell. He couldn't make out much, except for the steady dripping of water somewhere to his left. The whitewashed wall alongside the door reflected only the slightest glimmer of light into the long, narrow block, leaving Jack with no more than an impression of the space ahead. It was enough. He hated this place so much it would be engraved on his mind forever.

'Just like you to hide in a place like this, Billy Murdoch,' he growled, hearing his voice resonate off the walls. 'A school toilet is just where you belong.'

He took a slow step forward, feeling every bump of the slippery, stone-flagged floor underneath the thin soles of his shoes. Gradually, his eyesight was becoming accustomed to the darkness. This end of the block was just an open space. Metal pipes on the wall and puddles of water reflected dimly in the distance. There was nowhere to hide along here.

Further along, then. In one of the stalls that occupied the

3

middle of the block, or over by the grubby sinks at the far end. He had seen Murdoch dart in at that end. There was no way he could have escaped.

'Maybe I'll dip your head down the pan, just like I did the first day I came here,' he said, as much to fill the dismal space with the sound of his own voice as to intimidate his quarry. 'That'll be before I knock your block off for stealing me dad's fruit . . .'

Still nothing. He groped his way across the damp floor towards the nearest of the stalls. As far as he could tell in this blackness, all the doors were closed. He reached out and tried the nearest with the toe of his shoe.

It creaked and fell open. The stall was empty.

'Did you think I'd not see you?' he challenged, becoming a little bolder as more and more of the room was revealed to his improving sight. He sniffed, and rubbed his forehead with his shirt sleeves. His hands felt clammy with excitement. Stepping up to the next stall, Jack tapped it open in the same manner as the first. Again, it was empty. Two to go.

'Or did you think you could just get away with it? Well, you're wrong, Billy. I'm never going to let you get away with anything. I'll always catch you. I'm bigger than you, I'm stronger than you . . .'

He kicked open the third door so that it banged against the wooden wall that separated it from the neighbouring stall.

'I'm going to make you sorry you ever met me, Billy Murdoch!' he roared, lunging at the fourth door confidently, knowing that there was only one place Billy could be hiding now . . . He heard the door crash back, and there was a moment when he felt triumphant, as he caught sight of Billy squirming along on the floor on his belly, trying to get under the partition into the next stall.

That moment didn't last very long. The thunderous crack of the door smacking back against the flimsy wall had been joined by a loud, metallic clatter from above. Jack looked up, but he almost knew what it was before it fell. A tatty tin bucket, which moments before had been balanced on the door, but which was now spinning round, falling, and throwing out a wide spray of icy water . . .

Jack was drenched. He managed to throw his hands up so that the bucket didn't land on his head, but there was no way to avoid being soaked. The water was freezing cold. It ran inside the collar of Jack's shirt, saturated his trousers, and plastered his hair down

4

to his head. *The shock was almost as solid as a fist.*

Jack was almost literally frozen to the spot. He could barely move, stunned by both the awful, biting chill of the water and the realisation that Billy had out-thought him. He had no doubt that the little thief would evade Tom. Billy would escape once again.

He wanted to shout, but all he could manage was a scream of rage as he remained rooted to the spot in the dismal darkness of the school toilets. In his head, though, he was calling out very loudly.

I'll get you, Billy . . . one day soon, I'll get you!!!!

Two

It was nearly the end of the day. It was nearly the end of term. More than that, though, it was nearly the most important day in Chris Stephens' life.

He couldn't stop thinking about it, so it was just as well that the last lesson on that Friday afternoon was double English, and that Mr King was allowing the class to work on some free writing while he sat at his desk, looking out of the window. Instead of taxing them with Shakespeare, some dreary dead poet or some modern writer who managed to waffle on for 50 pages about falling in love, Mr King was allowing his students the chance to daydream. Chris knew their English teacher was daydreaming as well. He had a boat, which he took sailing around the coast during the holidays. Soon, the summer vacation would begin, and Mr King would leave GCSE English, Spirebrook Comprehensive and the city of Oldcester far behind.

Just a few more days . . .

Chris had plans for the summer vacation as well, and they had nothing to do with boats. For starters, there was the second leg of an exchange scheme that had been arranged with an American school. Chris was looking forward to that. There was the prospect that he might have a part-time job at the same computer store his father worked at, which would allow him to earn some money for a change. That was good news too.

More important than either, though, was his appointment the weekend after this at the London Road training ground of Oldcester United, the team he had supported since he was just a kid. If all went well, after this summer he wouldn't have to daydream about football any more.

He would be living it.

The sheet of A4 paper in front of him was largely empty. He had been trying to find a way to express how he felt about the future. He couldn't. Ever since that first time his father had taken him to see Oldcester United play at Star Park, Chris had been captivated by football. He played for the school team – had been captain of the lower school side since the autumn; he also played for a local youth side, the Riverside Colts, who had recently been crowned champions of the Oldcester District League. Chris played every chance he could, anywhere, anytime.

And he was good. Above average height for his age, Chris was excellent in the air. He was also quick across the ground, with sharp reactions. But everyone said it was his balance, vision and two-footed shooting power that stood out. Chris was a natural goalscorer, able to see where chances might fall and get into position to take them. Even though the school team hadn't had a marvellous year, Chris had scored a lot of goals for them. He'd snapped up another sackload of goals for the Colts, including a hat-trick in the game just after Easter that had clinched the title.

There were plenty of people telling him he had a future in the game. Chris was starting to believe it.

Which was why the rapidly approaching appointment he had in eight days' time was so important. Each year, Oldcester United ran trials to find promising young players for its youth teams. Chris had taken part in a trial like that a year ago, and had narrowly missed making the grade. He knew he was a better player now. He hoped he was good enough.

There were big changes happening at Oldcester United and Chris wanted to be part of them. Rumours were flying that the reason the trials were being held so late this year (they were normally held at Easter) was that a major new sponsorship deal was going to be announced, which would include money for a School of Excellence along the lines of the youth scheme run at Ajax in Holland.

This would be more than just a bigger, better youth team set-up. It would be something new in English football. The players signed up to the scheme would go to a new school, owned and run by Oldcester United. It would be a real school with proper lessons and approved teachers, but it would ensure the boys followed a flexible training schedule.

Building work had already started on a new site just beyond Star Park, Oldcester's modern stadium on the river. The whole city was talking about it. A sponsorship deal would be the clincher.

Chris considered the prospect as he had done several times a day over the last few weeks. If all the rumours about the new school proved to be true, and if he got through the trials, this could be one of the last times he had to sit in Mr King's double English, one of the last times he ever came to Spirebrook Comprehensive as a student. *If* he was good enough ...

That, of course, was the question. Was he good enough?

Despite everything people had told him, and despite the thrilling season he had enjoyed, Chris couldn't quite convince himself that it was going to happen. Thinking about the trials made him giddy with nerves. He couldn't wait for them to start, but he was dreading them at the same time. Although there were all kinds of ifs and maybes, the main issue was simple enough. Was he a good enough player to make the grade?

Chris looked down at the sheet of paper again, as if he hoped that some words had appeared on the page magically. Still nothing. Perhaps football wasn't the best subject to write about. Perhaps he needed to think about something else, something equally important in his life. But what else was there?

Chris sighed and looked around. Even Nicky was writing something, which really showed Chris how brain-dead he was. Nicky normally took to creative writing like a duck to sky-diving, but today he was scribbling furiously, his eyes bright with concentration. Chris stole a glance round at some of the others in the class. Russell was working, Jazz was working ...

OK, OK, he thought. I have to get something down on this paper other than my name. And then it struck him. He could write about football, but stay away from his own confused feelings about the trials. There was one subject about which he knew exactly how he felt.

He started to write.

'A bit previous, aren't you?' asked Jazz.

Chris looked round to face his friend, not quite certain what Javinder Ray was talking about.

'Writing about Oldcester winning the Championship,' Jazz explained. 'Just because United have been promoted back into the Premier League doesn't mean they'll do anything. I mean, year before last they were relegated.'

Nicky, who shared Chris's passion for football, and who loved a pointless argument even more, butted in before Chris had thought of an answer.

'They'll not get relegated again. This is a better team than the one that went down. If I were you, I'd be much more worried about Chelsea.'

Jazz frowned, caught out by the speed with which Nicky had turned things round on him. Ever since Jazz had announced his decision to 'support' Chelsea, spurred on by watching the magic Ruud Gullit had brought to the side, Nicky had been on his case, mocking the choice. Nicky was one of those football fans who believed that you had to support your local team, even if that meant you were forever stuck with some outfit propping up the Third Division. He had no time at all for people who 'adopted' successful sides and never went to see them play.

Chris knew this particular argument could run and run. Tonight, he wasn't in the mood for one of Nicky's lectures (even if it was being delivered at someone else), so he came to Jazz's rescue, clattering the door of his locker closed to get their attention.

'What are you doing this weekend?' he asked.

Jazz wasn't cheered up by that subject either. 'I'm working in the shop tonight and tomorrow morning, then we have the match on Sunday . . .' Chris nodded. The Colts were playing in a summer Cup competition, in which the winners from different district leagues would meet up. Chris and Jazz, along with Mac and Russell Jones, were in the team for the first game, against a side from Wolverhampton.

Ordinarily, the match would have been uppermost in Chris's mind. The opposition in the tournament would be extremely good, including junior sides from some league clubs. It was quite possible that the Colts could go down at the first hurdle, and their season would be over. However, Chris was even more aware that — if things turned out the way he hoped — this might be his last game for the Colts anyway, win, lose or draw. If he signed for Oldcester United, he wouldn't be allowed to play for any other team.

Jazz hadn't been selected for the trials. After this weekend, they could be going their separate ways.

'Would your dad let you come to the Oldcester game on Saturday?' Chris asked. He caught Nicky's slightly surprised expression from the corner of his eye. It wasn't the first time a spare ticket had been offered, but Jazz always had to turn them down. It looked as if he was going to on this occasion as well.

'I don't think so, Chris . . .' he began.

Chris knew all the reasons Jazz normally trotted out whenever he was asked, and this time he was prepared. 'Jazz, it's a friendly game — Sean Priest's benefit. There won't be any away supporters, there won't be any trouble. Almost everyone else from the Colts is going . . .'

Jazz hesitated. Chris knew he wouldn't be keen to bring the subject up with his father yet again.

'I'll think about it.'

'Good,' said Chris. 'Give me a call.' He thumped Jazz on the back. 'It's about time you saw some real football.'

'I watch plenty —'

Chris cut him off. 'That's on TV. It's not the same.'

He was trying to make a genuine point, but Nicky pitched in to suggest that if Jazz went to some live games, he'd recover from his 'illness' of supporting Chelsea. With that, all rational discussion came to an end. Nicky managed to attract others into the argument. Since it was the closed season, supporters of every team in the Premiership were starting on an even footing, putting the case for their team to capture some silverware in the new campaign.

Chris found himself drawn into defending the fact that Oldcester hadn't yet dipped into the transfer market to bolster their squad. It seemed as if every other team in the country was signing up star internationals from Germany, Holland, Spain and Italy, and filling up their squads with bewildered Eastern Europeans and Africans. Oldcester had their Dutch midfielder, Piet van Brost, but he had been with the club so long that he spoke with a local accent.

'Lively's looking at someone special . . .' he insisted, drawing on yet another rumour that had been circulating for weeks. Dennis Lively, Oldcester's larger-than-life millionaire chairman, was supposed to have been visiting Europe, investigating the possibility of capturing a big name. It didn't sound like Oldcester, who had more home-grown players than just about anyone in the League and who seemed to hang on to some old hands for what seemed like decades, but the rumours wouldn't go away.

Like all the best football arguments, this one didn't actually change anyone's opinion or prove anything. The group – which had grown to include about ten boys and two teachers – gradually drifted away, heading for the exits.

Chris and Nicky left the school grounds together, using the back gate out on to the new road that led through the retail park. It was a short cut to get to Nicky's place, where they planned to spend an hour or two before Chris's father got home.

As they walked along the pristine white pavement, past the newly bedded plants and the road signs that hadn't seen even a touch of graffiti, Chris took a look back through the fence at the school. It was nagging at him that he might not see this familiar sight many more times; the ugly, low teaching buildings, all glass and grey concrete; the battered old gym; the boiler room; the dining hall . . . and, most of all, the broad, sweeping field, which looked as if it was pinned to the ground by the massive pylons that marched across it. Two of the monsters sat on either side of the football pitch, cables strung high above one penalty area. Chris and Nicky had challenged each other to be the first to kick a ball over the wires. It seemed a long time ago.

And now, there were just two days left of term . . .

Nicky saw him looking back, and caught the moody expression on Chris's face. Not for the first time, he managed to completely misread what he saw there.

'Just think,' he said, 'after Saturday we might be rid of this dump for good!'

'Yeah,' said Chris in a low voice.

Three

Saturday morning was bright and hot. Forecasts suggested that the temperature could be 25 degrees by the afternoon. Chris woke up early, dimly aware of the last echoes of a weird dream in which he had been signed from Lazio by Dennis Lively for £20 million, and introduced to the media as Oldcester's new signing.

The sun was already shining over the street outside. Chris dressed quickly and made his way downstairs to the kitchen. His father was sitting at the breakfast bar, the kettle boiling on the counter behind him. He was concentrating on the newspaper he had propped up in front of him. As soon as he saw Chris, he lifted the paper so that Chris could see the back page.

'Take a look at this,' was all he said by way of introduction.

The top half of the page was dominated by a picture of Dennis Lively holding up a shirt in Oldcester's familiar colours, but which was very different from the red and blue stripes they had worn for as long as anyone could remember. The body of the shirt was red and the sleeves were blue, in the same vein as the kit Aston Villa or West Ham wore (only the colours were louder). And written across the shirt's breast in bold white lettering was a new sponsor's logo — two words picked out in white, one in a kind of handwritten style with a bold slash underneath.

'Virgin Cola?' read Chris. The newspaper headline writer obviously must have had trouble believing it too, since he had written '£10,000,000 FOR OLDCESTER SOCCER VIRGINS'.

'Some new sponsorship deal,' his father explained quickly. 'Virgin Cola are going to put money into this new soccer school, plus they get to put their name on the first team shirts.'

There was more of the story inside, and Chris went round to sit beside his father and skim through the story.

'But I thought they already had money for the school,' said Chris, who thought he was as up to date on the subject as he could be. He knew that contractors had knocked down some old terraced housing further along Easter Road to make room for the new building. Work had already started on the foundations. There was a special display in the club shop and the local newspaper had been publishing details on a week-by-week basis. It was the most important move the club had ever made.

'It says Virgin Cola are going to be supplying equipment for the school; computers and suchlike,' Mr Stephens said. 'Plus they're putting in some extra money to help the club secure its place in the Premiership. I'm sure there'll be more about it at the ground today. Sean's bound to be in the know.'

Chris started to feel a tingle of excitement. Oldcester had lacked a big-name sponsor in the past. Perhaps this would put them into a better position to challenge the big guns, like Liverpool, Manchester United and Newcastle.

His dad was right; if anyone would be able to tell them what was going on it would be Sean Priest, the youth development manager at United. An ex-player with United, Sean had come back from a spell on the Continent with Rotterdam to take over coaching Oldcester's future stars. He also kept a close eye on the Colts. It was widely known that Priest had set up the Colts to have a reserve pool of players he could keep an eye on. He had been keeping a particularly close eye on Chris.

'Well,' Mr Stephens said, laying down the paper and reaching for the teapot. 'We'll ask him later. I'm looking forward to this game, you know.'

Small wonder. Chris's dad had worked every Saturday since the end of the season, making up for the Saturday afternoons he took off to see United's home games. Even though this afternoon's match was only a friendly – a benefit for Sean Priest and a chance to publicise the new school – Chris knew his father couldn't wait to take his seat in the Easter Road Stand.

'What are your plans for this morning?' he asked, looking puzzled when he found there was no tea in the pot. The paper must have interrupted him after he put the kettle on. Chris grinned privately.

'I'm not sure,' he replied. He wanted to get a few things done on the computer, and then he and Nicky had a loose arrangement to meet over at Memorial Park at 11am. There were often groups of kids from different schools playing football there on a Saturday. Maybe they'd get a game going.

'I'll meet you in town, then,' his father said. 'Two pm. Outside Burger King.'

'Fine.'

Satisfied that everything was arranged, Chris's father started the tea-making process in earnest while Chris read the article in the paper. He looked across at the bottle of cola on the worktop. Sunday was supermarket day. Perhaps he should suggest to his father that it was time they changed brands . . .

As Chris stepped out through the door later that same morning, he felt the air wrap round him like a warm blanket. The sun was already pretty fierce and the street seemed alive with birdsong and distant voices. Cars were being washed, lawns mowed. It was a day for being outdoors. Locking the door securely behind him, Chris shouldered his bag and jogged to the top of the road to catch a bus.

The weather matched Chris's mood perfectly. Friday's damp, dull cloud had been replaced by a cloudless sky and glaring sunshine. He'd forgotten the empty feeling that had gripped him whenever he thought about leaving Spirebrook and his friends behind; he'd forgotten the anxiety that gripped him whenever the trial popped into his mind.

The next eight days were going to be among the most exciting he could ever hope for. He was determined to enjoy them.

The bus arrived just a few minutes after Chris arrived at the stop, which proved that it was a good day. Traffic through Spirebrook was often jammed up tight because of the new supermarket at the other end of the main road, so the bus timetable was something of a local joke.

It took about fifteen minutes to reach Memorial Park, which lay just inside the ring road, about halfway between

Oldcester city centre and Spirebrook, the district where Chris and Nicky lived. The streets around the park were filled with large, detached houses. Chris had once been told that two or three of Oldcester's players lived round this way, so he and Nicky had adopted Memorial Park as a place to come, in the naïve hope that one day one of United's stars might come out and join in a kick-about. Chris took a long look at each house as he passed, trying to work out which ones might be the homes of his idols. There was one with a smart green Beamer in the drive; he figured that had to be one.

He passed through the large, decorative gates and into the park. He had no idea what Memorial Park was a memorial to, since there was nothing written on the gates and no signs. However, on a day like this, it was a great place to be.

Several hundred other people seemed to have had the same idea.

Just about every part of the park was filled with people. There were queues outside the tennis courts, on which doubles and singles matches of varying quality were taking place. It was the same every year. Wimbledon came on the TV and suddenly everyone was Greg Rusedski. A few weeks ago, Chris and Nicky had been playing football-tennis on those courts and hadn't seen more than one other pair of players all morning . . .

It was the same on the mini-golf course and the boating lake. People had turned out by the score to take advantage of the first hot day of summer.

Some of them were playing softball or cricket. Chris thought he recognised some of the latter group – some older kids from his own school, including Griff, who had been the captain of the lower school football team before Chris. For a brief moment, Chris thought about wandering over and asking to join in, but his cricketing skills were on a par with . . . well, on a par with some England cricketers, actually. Chris had decided long ago that cricket wasn't his game; it was best to stick to something he was good at.

Besides, if Nicky was here, he would be over on the other side of the gardens. Chris knew better than to leave Fiorentini waiting. Nicky's volatile temper was legendary. Chris had been on the wrong end of it more than once.

He looked around. Heat haze drifted up from the paths, giving everything a dream-like quality. Voices drifted across the grass, sounding squashed and muffled, but still carrying over large distances.

As he crossed the broad strip of grass between the tennis courts and the formal gardens, Chris delved into his bag and fetched out the ball he had brought. He dropped it on to his instep as he shouldered the bag again, then broke into a run, dribbling the ball ahead, keeping it under tight control. As he got closer to the fence, he stroked a firm drive so that the ball hit the railings and came back at him. A perfect one-two. Nicky couldn't have played it better.

'And the railings don't mind if I'm a few minutes late, either . . .' muttered Chris, picking up the pace. He reminded himself that the trials next weekend started pretty early; he'd better make sure he was up in plenty of time.

Once again, he felt a twinge in his stomach and a prickling feeling as the hairs on the back of his neck stood on end. Just thinking about the trials had brought back all his nervousness about the big day. Even in the scorching heat of the sun, it was almost as if a chill breeze had touched his skin.

For the first time, he started to think that he would be glad when the trials were all over. Having to prove himself against the best players in the area was one thing, but all this waiting was doing his head in. He wished he could put it all to one side, but his mind kept racing around the possibilities. Was he good enough? Could he pass the test?

The sound of someone's harsh voice shouting brought Chris back to reality, back to the here and now. He looked up, surprised to find that he had wandered into the gardens without realising it. He stopped walking, trying to figure out where the voice was coming from. The air was so thick, everything sounded slowed down, like a video being played at the wrong speed. The voice, a really ugly, brutish yell, could have been coming from some way off, or from just behind the nearest hedge. It was hard to be sure.

'Come back here!' the voice demanded. Chris whirled round, thinking that whoever it was was behind him. There were scuffing, running footsteps coming closer, somewhere beyond the tall rose bushes . . .

Chris was almost startled as a small, scruffy figure came hurtling around a corner in the path, boots skidding on the surface. The boy was about Chris's age, or maybe a year or two younger – it was hard to tell. He was wearing heavy boots – Doc Martens, maybe – and a baggy white shirt, the end hanging loose outside his long shorts.

His hair was short, combed over from a severe parting. He looked tall, but as skinny as a rake. There was a look of alarm in his eyes.

The near/distant voice boomed again: 'I mean it! Come back, or I'll –'

The unspoken threat seemed to spur the young lad on even faster. He was racing towards Chris, breathing rapidly, almost falling over as he tried to pick up his tired legs. If the owner of the angry voice was close behind, Chris had no doubt that the boy wouldn't stay ahead of him for long.

With the possible exception of some arch-supporters of the big clubs, there isn't a football fan in the country who doesn't have a soft spot for the underdog. This sometimes disappears when their team gets drawn against a non-League team in the third round of the FA Cup, but most supporters of teams like Southampton, Norwich, Sheffield United or West Ham get as much pleasure from seeing the likes of Bury win at Anfield or Elland Road as they do when their own teams win.

Supporting a team like Oldcester United, you had to have a soft spot like that. Half the time, they were the underdogs themselves.

Chris was typical of that kind of fan. When the third round of the Cup was drawn, he prayed for some part-timers from the GM Vauxhall Conference or the Beazer Homes League to be given the chance to take out one of the really big names.

All of which goes some way to explain why he reached out as the lad went past, grabbing at his sleeve and pulling him into the shelter of a large bush (or small tree, Chris had no idea which), whose leafy branches curved down from the trunk to the ground, creating a small, shady hiding place inside. The boy uttered a small yelp of alarm as he was grabbed, but he didn't offer any greater protest than that. Chris took a moment to check that the boy was lying still and quiet, then positioned himself at the gap in the foliage.

'Keep down!' he urged, looking back along the path. He waited to see what kind of monster would appear in pursuit and tried to think how he was going to handle things if he was blamed for the boy's disappearance. He was already starting to wonder if this impulsive action was going to prove to be such a good idea.

No-one appeared. Chris listened carefully, still certain that whoever was chasing the boy would appear at any moment. What would he do then? The best plan Chris could devise was that he was going to say 'he went that way', and point off along the path (though he was sure that never worked, even in movies). His mind raced in pursuit of better ideas, but none came.

Fortunately, neither did any sign of anyone chasing along the path.

'Keep still,' Chris whispered from the side of his head, not risking looking down. 'I'll see what's happening.'

Trying to appear casual, he walked to the corner of the path. Still no-one. A short distance beyond the turn, the walkway opened out into a neat central space, in which there was an ornamental fountain and some iron seats. There was no sign of anyone at all, least of all some hulking bully. Chris breathed a sigh of relief, strolling over to the fountain. Water played from the mouth of a dolphin, trickling into the bowl. It made Chris thirsty.

There was a small confectionery stall on the other side of the garden. Chris decided to get himself a drink. First things first, though. He turned back along the path to the tree/hedge, ducking his head to look under the branches.

'You can come out now, he's go—' he started to say.

The boy had vanished. Chris was staring into an empty space.

He straightened and looked around. He was alone. All he could hear was birdsong and – just – the distant splattering of water from the fountain.

'Please,' he said loudly. 'Don't bother to thank me!'

There was no answer. The boy was gone. And so was Chris's football.

Four

— ⚽ —

It took Chris a moment to realise that he didn't have it. He could vaguely recall letting the ball roll to a stop at the edge of the path, just a little further along from the hiding place he had pulled the boy into.

He checked along the path in both directions, but he was already perfectly sure what had happened. The ungrateful little toad had stolen it! After Chris had saved his neck!

'Unbelievable!' he roared, kicking at some loose chippings in frustration. The pieces of bark scattered among the bushes.

'Hey! Mind the plants!' came a voice. Chris almost leapt out of his skin. He whirled round quickly, wondering if he had been sprung by the park keeper, or by whoever had spooked the boy.

It was neither. A man had appeared on the path, at the corner leading to the fountain. Chris blinked as he looked at him – there was a bright shaft of sunlight filtering through the branches of a tree behind the man's dark-haired head. He stepped forward, allowing Chris to see him a little bit more clearly.

'I didn't harm any plants,' Chris retorted, then he added, 'Some kid just stole my ball.' It struck him at once that the two sentences didn't quite fit together, but it was too late now.

The man gave him a broad smile, obviously amused by Chris's outburst. Actually, now that Chris could see him more clearly, he realised that the new arrival wasn't as old as he'd first guessed – maybe just nineteen or so. The guy had bright blue eyes, and his face was pale and clear. He had shiny black hair, cut short in a pretty brutal way, except for a bit of a fringe which flopped over his forehead in the same way as Nicky's always did.

'Maybe it's still here,' the guy said. Chris grunted, pretty sure he'd looked everywhere, but he still joined in as the man looked through some plants, lifting leaves and branches with his heavy black boot.

The change in the weather must have caught a few people by surprise, Chris decided. His feet felt hot just in trainers.

'Is this it?' the man said suddenly. He reached into a thick patch of . . . well, some green stuff Chris couldn't name, and pulled out the ball. Chris was amazed. How had it rolled so far?

'Thanks! Looks like I owe the kid an apology.'

'Not to mention the plants,' said the man, smiling, with a nod in the direction of the flowers Chris had showered with bark. Chris grinned sheepishly.

The man was testing the ball between his hands, feeling the pressure with his fingertips.

'Feels pretty light,' he said, frowning. He bounced it twice on the path.

'It should be OK,' said Chris. 'I pumped it up before I came out.'

The guy nodded in acknowledgement, but his concentration remained fixed on the ball. He tossed it up lightly, took it on his thigh, dropped it down on to his instep and knocked it back up to his hands, all in one fluid movement.

'Do you play?' he asked Chris.

'Sure,' Chris replied, impressed by what he had seen. 'I play for my school team and for another side on Sundays. We practise Wednesdays.' He decided not to add 'and I'm going out of my mind wondering if I'll pass a trial with Oldcester United next weekend'. He wondered if the guy played.

At that point, Chris noticed that the shirt the man was wearing was a replica of some old United shirt, with broad red and blue stripes and the club badge in the centre of the chest. It looked really old-fashioned, with a lace-up collar and everything. Chris thought it was pretty neat, even if it wasn't a proper version of the United strip.

The strip United were about to abandon, Chris reminded himself.

The man was also wearing some highly fashionable (and completely naff) baggy white shorts. If it wasn't for the heavy black boots, Chris would have guessed he was on his way to a game. Instead, Chris decided he was just a very keen fan with plenty of money to buy replica kit and no dress sense. Chris wasn't a great believer in football kit as fashion wear.

The man was watching Chris every bit as closely as Chris was watching him. Then he said, 'Come and show me what you can do', and turned away, walking towards the centre of the gardens.

Chris opened his mouth to say something, but no words came out. He ran his hand through his thick mop of blond hair and set off to follow the man. After all, it was his ball . . .

Chris started off in the belief that they were going to go out through the gate on the other side of the gardens, which suited him OK since that was the way he'd been heading anyway. His father had always told him to avoid strangers, but he wasn't a five year old any more. A couple of minutes kicking a ball around until Nicky arrived couldn't land him in any trouble, could it?

However, the man didn't go any further than the space around the fountain before he dropped the ball. He paused to tie his laces, then stood up with the ball at his feet.

'We can't play here,' said Chris automatically, looking around. 'It's not allowed. If the park keeper –'

'Do you always do everything you're told?' the man laughed. Chris felt his face flush a little.

'No . . .'

'Come on, then. There's no-one around, and it's not like we're going to damage anything. See if you can get the ball off me.' He had a confident, broad smile on his face that suggested he didn't think that was very likely.

'Can't we do this on the grass outside?' asked Chris. After all, it was only a few yards away.

'I have to stay here,' the man replied sharply, looking around.

'Are you supposed to be meeting someone?' asked Chris. The man turned his head back to face him very slowly. The smile had vanished for a moment, but it slowly came back.

'It's just that . . .' he said in a low, husky voice, '. . . just that there are some things I have to do.' He looked up at the sky briefly, then fixed his eyes back on Chris. He clapped his hands twice, the cocky grin returning.

'You want your ball back, don't you?' he said, taunting Chris.

'I don't know . . .' Chris replied. He'd had a good patch of not being in trouble with anyone for anything. He wasn't at all sure he wanted to spoil it just to provide this guy with five minutes entertainment.

'Come on! Don't be such a baby. Come and get your ball back!'

Chris dropped his bag on one of the iron benches.

'Fine,' he replied. 'Let's do it.'

Tackling wasn't one of the strong points of Chris's game, and the man had a few years and several inches of height advantage over him. All the same, Chris didn't see how it could be so difficult. In those boots, his opponent would be lucky to stay upright, let alone run around.

Besides, Chris wasn't prepared to let that smug smile stay in place for another second.

The man rolled the ball out from under his right foot and started to dribble towards Chris, who was still on the outside of the circle. Chris stepped up quickly, shutting down the space between them. The ball jumped out in front of his opponent, tantalisingly close to Chris's left foot. He stretched out to take it.

He never made contact. Moving like lightning, the man stretched out and snatched it away, turning sharply to his left. It was all Chris could do to avoid falling.

'You'll have to do better than that,' the man laughed, moving off around behind the fountain, the ball tightly controlled with what seemed like delicate, stroking touches off the end of the heavy boot. Chris watched him circle the fountain and moved into the centre of the path as the man completed his lap. He clenched his teeth and balanced himself ready to challenge.

The man was picking up speed, still dribbling the ball closely. His arms were outstretched for balance, and his head was down over the ball at almost every step. His size made him quite a daunting prospect to take on, but Chris thought he had the guy's measure. So far, he hadn't once used his left peg. Chris positioned himself, ready to take advantage of that fact.

The ball was skipping over the floor as the man got close. Chris turned sideways, backing off a little, shadowing his opponent's moves.

Just as he'd hoped, he forced the guy inside, towards the fountain. Now he stepped up, closing him down, trying to trap him quickly before he could adjust. If he couldn't use his left foot, he'd be easy meat.

The ball was there to be taken. Chris closed in the final step and prepared to cut across the man's path.

In that same instant, the guy reached out with his right foot, pulling the ball back with the inside of his boot. Flicking the ball behind his left foot, he pivoted around 270 degrees, collected the ball again, and was behind and away from Chris in what seemed like a split second.

'How did he do that?' Chris asked himself, a moment before his backside hit the path with a very respectable thump. 'Ow!'

The man looked back as he heard Chris cry out. For a moment, he wore the maddeningly confident grin that was threatening to tee Chris off in a big way, but then it faded and he looked almost sorry for what he'd done.

Chris was feeling pretty sorry for himself too. The guy had spun him round like a top. He hadn't been made to look this foolish for a long time. He sat still, recovering his poise, breathing hard even though the exercise hadn't lasted long enough to wind him. He could have been very angry indeed.

But he wasn't. Instead, he started to find the whole thing ridiculous. Without really understanding why, he began to laugh.

The man came up, offering his hand to help Chris up. Chris was still laughing out loud as he was pulled to his feet.

'Sorry,' said the man, 'I didn't mean . . . that is, I didn't think . . .'

Chris told him not to worry about it. 'You were just too good for me. Of course,' he added defensively, 'tackling isn't the strong part of my game.'

'No? What do you do?'

'I play up front,' said Chris. The man appeared puzzled for a moment until Chris added, 'I've been top scorer for Spire-brook the last two years.'

'Ah! I like to play full back. Perhaps I should have tried to tackle you!'

Chris grinned back. The guy might have looked like a bit of a clown in his antique gear, but he was all right. He reminded Chris a little of Sean Priest, who never sounded as if he was talking down to younger players. It wasn't something many adults managed.

'I thought you must have played before. Was it in the League?'

The man beamed with pride. 'Aye, it was. A long time ago.'

'Who with?'

The man's eyes were focused on a distant place, it seemed to Chris. Perhaps he was remembering his playing career. Something pretty drastic must have happened for it to have finished already. Chris still had the bloke pegged at being no more than twenty.

Suddenly, the guy's attention snapped back to the present. 'Are you any good with your head?' he asked. Chris nodded enthusiastically. 'Right . . .' the man said, grinning and stepping back. 'Let's see how long we can keep this thing in the air.'

With that, he tossed the ball up, waiting for it to fall before he snapped his head forward. The header was perfectly weighted and the ball flew in a gentle arc to where Chris was waiting. Bracing his neck muscles, Chris popped the ball back. They managed ten headers like that before the ball fell to the ground. At the second attempt, they managed 30. Chris felt like they could have broken the hundred with just a little more time.

'You're pretty good . . .' the man said at last. Chris was puffing genuinely now. He'd worked hard to keep up with his partner, who seemed determined to keep the game alive for as long as possible.

'I hope so,' said Chris. 'I've got a trial next weekend. With Oldcester United.' He felt a little guilty for showing off, but the words had popped out before he could stop them. His new friend seemed delighted.

'My old team!' the man laughed. He clapped Chris on the shoulder.

'You played for Oldcester?' Chris replied, completely taken off-guard.

The man's smile faded. He looked up into the sky. 'Yes. It was something I'd always dreamed of. I never thought my chance would come.'

Chris knew what he meant, but something more important was nagging at him. 'I'm not being funny, but I don't recognise you. When was this?'

The man's expression changed to one of sadness. 'A while ago, now,' he said. 'It wasn't a very long career.' He blinked against the sunlight before looking back down at Chris. Were those tears in his eyes, or had he just blinded himself with the sun? 'Let's hope you do better, eh? When's this trial, you say?'

'Next weekend.'

'Listen, do you fancy a bit of extra practice? I'd be glad to help out. Maybe I could teach you how to tackle a bit better.'

'I could use it,' said Chris.

'Well, good. Meet me here tomorrow afternoon –'

'I've got a game tomorrow.'

'Afterwards, then. I'll meet you here, OK?'

Chris avoided meeting the man's direct gaze while he took a moment to think it over. He wasn't quite 100 per cent sure about the guy, but there was no doubt he could play. In Chris's eyes, anyone involved with football couldn't be a wrong 'un, certain managers and agents excepted. Maybe, while they worked, Chris could get a few more answers . . . there were certain things that just didn't add up.

'OK,' he said at last.

The man seemed genuinely pleased. 'Great! I'll see you then!' He grinned once more and gave Chris a cheery wave. He was starting to turn away as Chris called out.

'Hang on – what's your name?'

'Eh?'

'I'm Chris Stephens. What do I call you?'

'Oh, right!' the man replied. 'My name's William.'

Five

—— ⚽ ——

William disappeared out of sight almost as suddenly as he had arrived. Chris found himself alone on the path, slowly recovering his breath. His mouth felt dry and parched. Time for a drink.

He walked over to the bench to get his bag and then turned to collect the ball. It was like a slap in the face when he realised that he couldn't see it.

'Not again!' he moaned out loud.

William hadn't walked off with it, he was sure of that. And there hadn't been another soul around. It must have just rolled somewhere.

Chris started poking through the bushes and plants at the edges of the path once more, feeling hot and bothered. There was a much bigger area to search this time and no-one to help. Chris felt himself becoming more and more frustrated by the minute.

It occurred to him that maybe there was someone who could help, assuming Nicky had arrived. Dropping the branch in his fist back into place, Chris hoisted his bag on to his shoulder and jogged past the fountain towards the far gate. If nothing else, he needed a drink badly. He was feeling quite lightheaded.

As he approached the far gate, he could hear some kids laughing and squealing. A harassed adult was calling them. The air was getting drier and hotter and Chris puffed out a deep breath, reaching the gate just as a young couple were walking through. Outside, the grass was dotted with blankets and rugs, and the area outside the small confectionery shop was crowded with people. A lot of them were in shorts and T-shirts; a few brave souls were wearing bathing costumes. It was more like sunny Spain than Oldcester.

26

'Hey, Chris!'

Chris looked up to see Nicky stalking across from the shop, clutching a can of Diet Pepsi. Chris could already tell from the tone of his voice that he had been waiting for some time.

'Let's have a sip, Nicky,' he said, reaching for the can. Nicky moved to snatch it away, but Chris was too quick for him. He drained the half-filled tin in two or three swallows.

'Help yourself,' said Nicky sourly as Chris handed it back to him.

'I'll buy us some more,' said Chris, stepping past him towards the store. Nicky followed him, watching as Chris fetched a fiver from his pocket and marched into the shop.

'Two Virgin Colas, please,' Chris asked the gum-chewing girl behind the counter.

'We don't have none,' she replied, not even bothering to look at him. 'Coke or Pepsi.'

'Neither. Two Orange Tangos –'

'They're in the chill cabinet,' she said, airily waving a hand which seemed to be covered in rings and bangles. Chris managed to find the cabinet, selected the drinks and paid for them. Nicky looked at his can in disgust.

'They out of Pepsi?' he moaned.

'Yes,' said Chris automatically. He was already snapping back the ring-pull.

'I hate this stuff . . .' muttered Nicky, while he watched Chris drain the can as quickly as he had emptied the first. Chris wiped the back of his hand across his mouth and took a long, deep breath. Nicky handed him the second can.

'I'm all right for the minute,' said Chris.

'I should think so!' Nicky said, pouting. He pushed back a stray lock of his wavy black hair. 'What have you been doing to get so thirsty?'

'Playing football.'

That wasn't an answer Nicky was pleased to hear.

'Really? I was going to have a game myself this morning, only my mate didn't show up.'

Chris looked across and grinned sheepishly.

'Sorry, Nicky. Look, I need a favour . . .'

'"Sorry, Nicky, I need a favour?"' Nicky repeated (almost

word for word), as if he couldn't believe his ears. 'Why do I put up with you?'

'Because I'm the only one who'll put up with you. Come on, Nicky. Lend us a hand – I've lost the ball.'

He stalked off back towards the gardens with Nicky in tow. Fiorentini was struggling to keep up – with Chris or the conversation.

'So you've been playing already? Is that why you're so hot? I thought you were going to faint or something.'

'I was just knocking the ball around with this bloke –'

Nicky was mortally offended. '*Bloke*? What "bloke"?'

'I'm not sure . . . he helped me find the ball.'

'Eh? I thought you said you'd *lost* the ball!'

'That was the second time. The first time, this guy appeared and helped me find it. Then we knocked the ball around for a while –'

'Until it got lost again,' Nicky concluded.

'Not quite,' said Chris as he reached the gate into the garden. 'Come on, this way.'

They walked along the path towards the fountain, retracing Chris's route. Nicky slowly fell behind as Chris pushed on, his hands shoved into the pockets of his shorts. He was muttering to himself. Chris gathered that Nicky had been waiting for quite a while.

'So, who was this geezer anyway?' asked Nicky, who seemed to have adopted this strange way of speaking after watching the second series of *Thief Takers*.

'Well, that's what was so weird about it,' said Chris. 'He said his name was William, and that he used to play for United!'

That piece of news grabbed Nicky's attention. Nicky loved rubbing shoulders with celebrities from the football world. He jogged to catch up with his team mate.

'Really? William who?'

'He didn't say.'

'Did you recognise him?'

Chris had stopped near the fountain, looking around as if he was in a dream. He was looking at all the people who were poking around trying to read the small signs that said what plants were what, or sitting on the benches. He looked surprised to see them.

28

'Did you recognise him?' Nicky asked again.

'No,' Chris replied, shaking his head slowly for emphasis. He still seemed quite distracted. 'Which is odd, really, because he only looked twenty-odd. Not very old at all.'

Nicky closed his eyes and screwed his face up as he tried to access the part of his brain in which he stored soccer trivia. Ask Nicky about any Oldcester home game over the last ten years and he'd rattle off the eleven names (and probably the subs) nine times out of ten.

'Nah!' he said. 'He must have been having you on. I can't remember a William after Bill Salmon, that bald centre half we had in the seventies.'

He opened his eyes and looked round for Chris, who was poking around in the foliage on the edge of the path.

'Now what?' he asked.

'I'm looking for the ball!' replied Chris, impatiently.

Nicky was becoming more and more amazed with every passing moment. 'You were playing in here?' he asked, his voice cracking into a squeak as he spoke the last word. Chris didn't always do everything he was supposed to, but it wasn't like him to break the rules so blatantly.

'There was no-one around,' said Chris, looking back over his shoulder defensively. 'Anyway, it wasn't my idea.'

Nicky didn't like the sound of that. The only person who normally managed to take advantage of Chris was Nicky himself.

'This bloke, right?' he asked, with an unpleasant, disappointed twist in his lip.

Chris stood up, frustrated in his search among the flower beds. It just didn't seem possible that the ball could have rolled any further. He looked back towards the path from which he had first entered the area around the fountain, the place where he had first encountered William. Perhaps he should search there?

He heard Nicky cough and looked round. One of the gardeners who looked after this part of the park was approaching, pushing a barrow.

All things considered, this didn't seem like a good time to continue the search, and Chris certainly wasn't going to ask the guy to help him look for the ball. He'd just have to let it go for now and maybe come back later.

Nicky was now by Chris's side, eyeing him and the gardener with equal suspicion.

'Maybe this bloke took the ball.'

Chris shook his head, but Nicky wasn't prepared to accept his denial without an argument. 'No, listen, maybe he hid it, right? Behind his back or something. Up his shirt?'

Chris replayed the incident in his mind. The one thing he couldn't imagine was William with a hunchback. 'I really don't think so, Nicky.'

'No, come on, be fair. Which way did he go?'

Chris shrugged, but then pointed out the path the man had taken.

'Aha!' cried Nicky, triumphantly. Chris couldn't grasp what point he was getting at until Nicky shook his head in despair and added, 'That path doesn't lead anywhere.'

'Doesn't it?' asked Chris. He was tempted to tell Nicky that it had to lead *somewhere*, but decided against it.

'Well,' said Nicky. 'There's a statue or something up there somewhere, but you can't get out of the gardens that way.'

They stood there together for a moment, looking at the entrance to the path as if they expected William to reappear right there and then.

'Let's take a look,' said Chris.

'At the going down of the sun, and in the . . . something . . . we shall remember them.' Nicky stood back from the statue's plinth.

'Morning,' said Chris, filling in the missing word from memory.

'Huh.' Nicky snorted derisively. 'Doesn't look like too many people remember these guys. I bet no-one has visited this statue for years.'

Chris had to agree that the area around the statue looked completely uncared for compared to the rest of the gardens. The paving stones were tilted and uneven, with grass and weeds growing up between the cracks. The plants in the beds on either side of the statue were equally unkempt, littered with empty crisp packets. Tall trees filled the space with deep shadow, even in the midst of the day's bright sunshine. Much of the writing on the small column and its supporting plinth was faded so badly it was unreadable. The stone itself was dirty and soiled with bird droppings.

Even so, it didn't take a genius to work out that it was a war memorial. A steel-helmeted figure with a rifle over his shoulder and a heavy pack on his back stood boldly on the top of the column, gazing back over his shoulder. Chris guessed he was meant to be waiting for his comrades to join him.

'You think this is the memorial, as in Memorial Park?' asked Chris.

'Could be,' said Nicky, who was scuffing his feet through some of the rubbish at the back of the statue. 'Pretty sad, if it is.'

There were some names on the plinth, under a legend which read 'Heroes of the Great War'. Chris read through a small group of the names, which were better preserved than those above and below them. Three Smiths and a Smythe. He wondered if any of the Smiths were related.

'No sign of your mate William,' said Nicky.

No, thought Chris. Just a George, two Arthurs and a Ben. He realised just in time that Nicky was thinking about something else.

'He might have been living here though. You know, dossing out behind the statue, living off crisps and stuff.' He indicated a pile of more solid rubbish. 'There's even an old blanket.'

Clearly, Nicky had made up his mind about William. Chris sighed, and waited to be given the official explanation.

'That's what I reckon, anyway,' Fiorentini continued. 'He's just some poor nutter who hangs around the gardens. You know, care in the community. He pretends to be an ex-footballer when he talks to people, just so they'll like him. And he nicked your ball because . . .' His voice trailed away. Even Nicky was hard-pressed to make that connection.

'That's not it, Nicky. His clothes weren't tatty, like he'd been living rough. He had on one of those replica United shirts and it looked brand new. And he was only young . . . You didn't see him. He could play, he could really play.'

'Well, OK. Maybe he did play for someone before. Maybe they let him go because he went loopy.'

'Nicky!'

Fiorentini screwed his face up and brushed back his hair. 'OK, OK. But you have to admit that he was a bit odd, coming up to you like that.'

Chris couldn't deny that. However, he wasn't ready to cast William as the villain just yet.

'It doesn't prove he took my ball.'

Nicky's mouth opened as if he was prepared to continue to prosecute that idea, but then it clicked shut. He shrugged, grinned and put his arm over Chris's shoulder.

'Fair enough. Either way, we don't have a ball, so there's no point hanging round here, is there? Maybe we can get a game with someone else?'

'I saw Griff outside,' said Chris.

'There you are, then. Let's go.'

By the time they reached the far gate, Nicky had completely forgotten about William. He had been chattering on about that afternoon's benefit game at Star Park, and was just shifting ground to the trial when Chris pulled up short, staring open-mouthed at a small group of young lads kicking a ball frantically between them in a game that owed more to pinball than football.

'I don't believe it . . .' he whispered.

It wasn't the most uncommon type of ball, but even so Chris thought it unlikely that a bunch of squealing seven year olds would have been given one to play with. He raced over the grass towards them.

'Hey!' he yelled. 'Where did you get that?'

The leader of the group was a freckled beanpole with dark hair and an expression that said he would lie if you asked him what day it was. His brow furrowed as he prepared to confront Chris, supported by the full weight of his pint-sized posse.

'In't yours,' he said. 'S'ours.'

'Did I say it was mine?' snapped Chris, impatiently. He scanned the group quickly, to see if any of them was the kid he had hidden earlier. No luck. 'I just asked you where you got it.'

'Tescos!' the boy replied. One of his mates giggled.

That satisfied Chris's mind; he was certain that it was his ball now. It was then he recalled there was even a way to prove it.

'Look, I know you didn't steal it, but that's my ball. It's got some marks on it. Next door's kid drew a face on it and you can still just about see where it is.'

The wide-eyed blond kid with the missing teeth who had giggled before looked down at the ball, which was lying at his feet. Even as Beanpole was snapping a defiant 'No, you can't!', No Teeth was bending down and asking 'Where?'

Chris showed him. No Teeth offered an apologetic giggle. Beanpole had magically transported himself to the back of the group, where he was trying to become invisible.

'We found it over by the fence,' No Teeth apologised, pointing off in a vague direction.

'That was lucky,' said Chris, trying to make it appear that he was grateful someone had found his ball for him. 'I bet you don't go in the gardens very often.' The fact was that he found the kid's story hard to believe. It was a long way from the fountain to the surrounding fence. Compared to what came next, though, that part of the story was perfectly straightforward.

'It wasn't in the gardens,' No Teeth said, puzzled. 'It was just there on the grass, by the gate.

'On this side of the fence.'

Six

'All right!' yelled Nicky. 'This is going to be brilliant!'

He was finding it difficult to keep still. There was a real buzz going round the stadium precinct. The food stalls were doing a roaring trade, but not half as much as the newspaper sellers. There had been some complaints, they heard, about the girls on rollerskates who were whizzing back and forth through the crowd giving away coupons for free cans of Virgin Cola. Then a large van arrived to make sure everyone had plenty of stock to give away.

Nicky was trying to catch the eye of a red-haired girl who had already given him two coupons. Chris hid a smile behind his hand.

It was unusual to get such a good gate at a friendly game, but all Oldcester was discussing the new sponsorship deal, the school and what it might mean. The local radio stations had been talking about little else, and they both had radio cars there, interviewing the growing numbers of people queuing up to buy tickets. The local TV news was setting up as well and the rumour was that a national BBC team were on their way to film a report for next Saturday's *Grandstand*.

The souvenir programme didn't have anything about the new sponsorship deal in it, but there was a long write-up about the new school. Chris read the first few paragraphs of the report, but it just reminded him about the trial on Saturday and how important it was. He put the programme in his pocket.

Nicky wasn't suffering in the same way at all. In fact, he was starting to look forward to the future a great deal (possibly, thought Chris, because he believed he would get free cans of drink from red-headed girls at every home game from now on). He was carrying a brightly coloured carrier bag containing a brand new computer game, *Player Manager 4*. They'd been to Futurezone to buy it on their way to the game. Chris hadn't been flush enough to afford anything, but Nicky had said they could go back to his house after the match to give it a spin.

'Goodbye Spirebrook Comprehensive!' Nicky called out, lifting his face to the heavens. 'No more 'Andy' Cole; no more Ms Robinson, no more –'

'There are still going to be teachers at this new school, Nicky,' Chris's father pointed out gently. Nicky ignored the fact. As far as he was concerned, the future was settled. He'd sail through the trials, get a place in the United youth team and start at the new school as soon as it was built. Every day, he'd train and play football for a few hours. He'd never have to set foot in Spirebrook Comprehensive or do geography again. Maybe he'd have to do some courses on sports medicine or management, but no-one would expect him to know the capital of Brazil – just how well they'd done in the World Cup.

A lack of self-confidence was never going to be one of Nicky's problems.

Chris, on the other hand, had almost missed the offer of his free coupon. He was daydreaming, about the trial, the school and the mystery of William. It was getting harder and harder to stay focused on anything else. His father looked at him with a little concern when he didn't even pester for food.

'You OK, Chris?' he asked.

Chris managed to wake up just enough to put on a bright smile and answer, 'Sure. I'm really looking forward to this.' A few weeks before, this would have been perfectly true. Today, Chris could barely register what was happening.

'Hey, look,' he heard Nicky exclaim. 'They've opened the museum.' The club's museum never opened on match days (in case visiting fans tried to pinch the silverware!), but the sign was out and the smart doors into the private part of the Easter Road Stand were open.

'Can we take a look?' asked Chris.

'There's nothing we haven't seen before, Chris,' said his father.

35

Chris nodded in agreement, but asked again anyway. His father looked at his watch. There was still a little time before kick-off and Chris had a determined glint in his eye.

Chris led the way into the stand. The smartly tiled hallway on the ground floor was lined with photographs from the recent past, but Chris went straight past them and started to climb the stairs to the museum. Nicky quickly worked out what was on his friend's mind and chased after him, whispering into Chris's ear as he drew alongside.

'Have you told your father about this morning?'

'What about this morning?' Chris replied, bluntly.

Nicky wasn't going to be brushed off. 'You know; that William geezer. Have you said anything about him to your dad?'

'No,' said Chris, in a tone that challenged Nicky to provide an answer to the unspoken question, 'Why should I?' Nicky rolled his eyes up, and sighed.

'Look, Nicky,' Chris explained patiently. 'This isn't the same as being ten years old and not going off with strangers. It was a public park, and I didn't got off anywhere with him. We just played football.'

Nicky was on the edge of arguing that this wasn't quite the whole story, but gave up and settled for a different approach. 'Are you hoping we'll find something about him in the museum?' he asked. 'But you said he was only in his twenties – how could we have missed him if he played over the last few seasons?'

The same thought had been troubling Chris ever since he'd spoken to William. Something was jabbing at him, demanding his attention. There was something he was supposed to have noticed.

'I thought we'd agreed he was just a harmless nutcase?' Nicky continued, seeing that Chris hadn't answered.

'You agreed,' Chris reminded him quickly. Nicky frowned. He agreed, they agreed – it never normally made any difference.

Chris didn't push the discussion any further. On many occasions, it was Nicky who pushed to get the answers to the mysteries they uncovered. But there was no point forcing him to get interested in something. With Nicky, you just went along with the flow.

The climb up to the museum was completed at last. Chris led the way in, the others trailing behind him as he headed for the spot he was looking for.

Oldcester United's museum was a small but bright affair, less a celebration of glorious victories than a homage to times passed. There was *some* silverware – the one FA Cup win in the fifties; the Autoglass Trophy from '93; a few divisional championships – but United hadn't achieved the ultimate prize of a League Championship. So, instead of endless cases of trophies and cups, there were some wonderful displays about different areas of the club's history and current activities.

One such area had inspired Chris ever since he had started coming to Star Park. It was a display showing the awards won by the United youth team a few years back, when Sean Priest had first taken over the reins. They'd achieved several wins in national and international tournaments between 1989 and 1994.

Several of those players were now making first-team appearances for United, while a couple had been sold on to bigger clubs. The last couple of years hadn't been quite so good, but the overall record was one of brilliant success.

Today, though, Chris ignored that end of the museum completely.

Instead, he was making straight for a board attached to a wall at the other end. On it were lists of names, around 30 under each heading, written directly on to a wooden board in black paint. Although the same handwriting appeared throughout, there were small differences, particularly at the end of each list.

The headings were seasons, starting with 1972/73 in the top left corner, leading up to the season just finished, halfway down on the right. The lists showed every player who had appeared for the first team over the last 25 years. As new players were transferred in, or went into the side from the youth team or the reserves, the sign-writer had been called in to add their names to the list.

Chris had read the board before. This time he studied it carefully.

There was a small problem; namely that the players' forenames were only given as initials. Chris worked down the

37

lines of single letters, looking for 'W's. There were only two, and Chris could name them both.

'Warren Pryce and Wallace McGregor,' said Nicky from behind him, coming to the same conclusion. 'No Williams.'

'Maybe he's a Bill, not a William,' said Chris. There were quite a few Bs. His finger trailed down the 1974/75 list. 'Look, there's Bill Salmon.' He started to read out some of the other Bs. Between the two of them they managed to remember the forenames of all but a couple.

'It could be that William isn't even his first name,' said Chris. 'Remember Paul Dunstand who played in goal back in the sixties?'

Nicky laughed. 'Yeah! His real name was something poncy like . . .' Nicky struggled to remember.

'Launcelot,' Chris said. 'Paul was his cousin's name, or something like that, and he borrowed it when he started playing football. Point is, would he be on here with an L or a P?'

'Dunno.' Nicky shrugged. He was looking at the list closely himself now, and Chris knew he was starting to get interested. He could almost hear the cogs turning as Nicky strove to work something out. 'Say you were out a bit. Say William was 30. In 1972 he'd be . . .' There was a long pause. Chris, though he'd worked it out, waited for Nicky to supply the answer. 'Five!' Nicky flicked back his hair and gestured at the board. 'If he ever played for United, it has to have been in the eighties or nineties. That means he would have to be on there somewhere.'

'That's what I figured.'

'Unless he's a fake,' Nicky added quickly, clearly remembering that he was supposed to be the one who didn't believe in William. Chris shot him a look out of the corner of his eye. 'Or maybe he only got into the reserves . . .' Nicky suggested, realising that his team mate wasn't happy with that first answer.

Chris stepped back from the board. 'We need to find someone who'd know who these other Bs are.' He turned and searched the room, but couldn't see anyone he recognised. 'Perhaps Sean will be at the Colts' game tomorrow,' he said. 'I'll ask him.'

Nicky seemed satisfied to leave it there and went over to a recently installed exhibition at the far end of the room. This particular cabinet contained various memorabilia that Sean Priest had collected over the years, which he was loaning to the club. Some time before, it had all been stolen from his car and Chris and Nicky had been lucky enough to get some of it back. They had been invited as guests of honour when the display was opened a couple of months back. Chris knew that Nicky had gone to look at himself in the press photographs that recorded the event.

Chris didn't follow his team mate. For one thing, the cabinet was right next to the exhibit about the new soccer school. Chris still found that even thinking about that made him sick with anxiety. More importantly, though, there was another way in which Chris might be able to track down some information about William.

Every decade of the club's history was documented and recorded in its own special display. Some of them were quite sad, in their own way. The 1940s case, for example, contained the names of those ex-players, coaches and staff who had given their lives in the Second World War. The 1960s case recalled some of the club's most depressing times, as United had slid from the First to the Third Division in four seasons and a fire had wrecked the old Rampart Stand, which had been a favourite with the home crowds before the new Star Park stadium was built. Chris remembered being told that fire had also claimed the original ground as well. Maybe the club was jinxed.

There were photos and other memorabilia, and Chris scoured the 1980s case on the off-chance that William appeared in it. No such luck.

Kick-off time was getting closer. Chris's father gestured to him, calling him over. It would take them a while to reach their seats and he didn't want to leave it to the last minute.

Chris walked back along the history cabinets, giving each a last glance as he passed. He was almost at the end of the row, near the door where his father was waiting, when something caught his eye. He stopped, stepped back and took another look. It took him a moment to recognise what it was that had triggered his interest. It turned out to be an old black and white team photograph from 1905 that had been hand-tinted to pick out the colours of the United kit. There was nothing familiar about any of the players, but there was about the shirts each wore proudly.

Chris took a moment to make sure, comparing the 1905 kit with that worn in the 1920s. He was right. Oldcester's familiar red and blue stripes were much thicker in the 1905 picture than those worn on the current shirts, which had stayed more or less the same from 1922 to the 1970s, when the first fashion changes occurred and sponsors' names had started to appear. The 1905 shirt was almost all red, with just a single, broad blue stripe down the middle and two more under the arms. No-one had worn a United shirt like that for over 80 or 90 years.

No-one, that is, except William.

Seven

⚽

Their voices were ringing in his ears. Thirty-five thousand packed into the ramshackle stands around the pitch, roaring on the two teams. It was like a dream; like a beautiful dream. The sun was warm on his face and he felt his heart beating thunderously. Every time he closed his eyes, he was scared that he would open them again to find himself somewhere else.

But it was always all right. Each time, as the bright sunlight filtered between his lashes in that last moment before they opened, the young man knew that he was where he belonged. This was the day he had waited his whole life for.

It was almost half-time. At his side, the manager was wrapped in a thick woollen coat, even though the sun was warm. Twice in the last few minutes, he had leapt to his feet to call instructions to his team. He was furious, his voice dark and throaty like thunder.

Thunder.

What had made the player think of thunder on a day like this?

'Come on, United!' yelled the manager. 'Wake up! They're making you look stupid. They're making us look bad!'

One of the second team players sitting behind the manager spoke up. His voice was cocky; full of bright good humour. The young man knew it was Albert, the B Team goalkeeper. United were 3–0 down. It was a good day to not be playing in the first team.

'Good heavens, Mr Forbes. It's only a friendly!'

Forbes, a heavy-set man with a shattered right leg and a reputation for being the most impatient manager in football, turned stiffly round on his good leg. His face, almost hidden under his hat and bushy moustache, was bright with rage.

'Just as well, Bassett, just as well. If we play as poorly as this *when the season starts, we'll be lucky to avoid a beating like this every Saturday!'*

'But it's not like we'll be playing the Spurs every week,' Bassett continued, wincing slightly as he saw Oldcester lose possession to a crunching tackle. The lads fell back in full retreat before another attack.

'You'll never play against them again with an attitude like that,' scolded Forbes. 'That's why I arranged this fixture, so you could see what a really good team can do.'

He paused and looked at the young man. As he did, the manager's fierce face took on an expression that was as close to kindly as he could manage.

'You want to think like young Billy, here,' he told Albert without honouring him with so much as a glance. 'You're busting to get on, aren't you, lad?'

'Yes, Mr Forbes!'

'Aye, well, it's all arranged. You'll take over at right back after half-time.' He threw a brown paper package on to Billy's lap; it smelled of soap and starch. Billy knew instinctively what it was. 'Keep an eye on their winger.'

The young man almost jumped to his feet there and then.

'You know I will, Mr Forbes.'

The giant moustache trembled as Forbes smiled. 'Aye, well, your moment will come soon enough.' He looked away then, up to the heavens as if he was trying to see outside the cramped confines of the ground. 'Make the most of it. Who knows, the way things are, you may never get the chance again.'

Billy took his seat, biting his lip impatiently. The grand clock with its Latin numbers, way across on the far stand, was showing twenty to four. Half-time couldn't be more than five minutes away. In just a quarter of an hour, he would be coming back out here clad in a freshly cleaned shirt of red and blue, ready to claim his place in the team.

Nothing could take that away from him.

The game was a riot.

Although it was only a between-seasons friendly, the crowd was pretty decent. They were all in good spirits, enjoying the carnival atmosphere of a warm afternoon. Before the game kicked off, Dennis Lively went out on to the pitch, followed by a large number of press photographers and TV camera operators. He had a couple of introductions to make, he said through the PA. One a surprise; one not.

The non-surprise came first. Mr Lively signalled for a tall, bearded man to step forward from the players' tunnel. Flashguns flashed, the crowd cheered and Richard Branson walked on to stand beside the United chairman. Some of the comedians in the crowd had clearly been expecting this, because a vast number of red and blue balloons suddenly floated on to the pitch. Most of them had the word Virgin written on them.

Branson and Lively were joined by the United manager, Phil Parkes, who was probably better known for his playing days at QPR and West Ham. The trio displayed the new United strip for the forthcoming season, holding up the shirt between them. It wasn't a shock to see it, of course, after the picture in the local paper, but this was the first time many people had seen the new kit in the flesh. The sponsor's logo stood out brightly on the dark red body of the shirt.

'Neat,' said Nicky.

Chris wasn't so sure. United had always played in stripes. Seeing them in a kit like this would take a lot of getting used to. A few old-timers in the seats around them offered the same opinion.

'Now for the second part of the announcement,' Mr Lively boomed. The PA suffered an instant attack of feedback. 'I'm pleased to say that, subject to getting him a work permit and some other legal nonsense, Oldcester United have joined the big names of the Premiership in attracting a player of the highest quality from overseas. The lad's arrived today, but he's a bit jetlagged so he'll not be answering any questions. Plenty of time for that before the season starts. He's got plenty to get used to about playing in England, but one thing he won't be troubled with is the colours he's going to wear. He's been playing in red and blue for a while now.'

The crowd was absolutely buzzing. Who did the boss mean? Parkes was grinning so widely that he looked as if his face might split. He was clearly very pleased with the signing. Who was it?

Dennis Lively had turned the new shirt round. On the back, in clean white lettering above the number 10, was the name Rodriguez.

'Oh my . . .' breathed Chris.

Not everyone else was as quick working out who it meant, but the word went round the stadium like electricity. Luis Rodriguez, the explosive Spanish international and Barcelona midfielder, was walking out on to the green grass of Star Park. He wore a sharp suit and his brooding, dark eyes flashed in every direction as he took in his new surroundings.

This guy was class.

'How much must they have paid to get him?' asked Nicky.

After a few brief pictures and handshakes, the non-smiling Spaniard walked back off the field with no more than a wave to the crowd in the Easter Road Stand. Everyone was left speechless.

'The queue for season tickets starts now,' Dennis Lively announced as he followed his new star from the field. Chris saw a few people actually rise from their seats and head for the stairs. They were OK; his father had booked for the new season at the last home game of the old one.

'Follow that,' Mr Stephens whispered. It certainly was one heck of an announcement.

The benefit game could have become a bit of an anti-climax after such a start, but the announcement just lifted the crowd even more. A few even hoped that Rodriguez might make an appearance.

He didn't, but plenty of other stars did. Instead of a conventional benefit match, Sean had arranged a game between his friends and his 'foes'. Organising the fixture had almost given him a nervous breakdown, but in the end, holding it in the closed season made it easier to get just about everyone he wanted. The match was played in a brilliant atmosphere and the crowd soon got behind the idea of cheering the 'Friends' and booing the 'Foes' like it was a pantomime.

In some ways it was. The Friends were mostly ex-team mates of Sean's – veterans now – along with some of the current United team and a tall, balding Dutchman from Rotterdam FC who looked about 40 but played as if he was nineteen. The subs bench – which was freely used during the match – contained more players with whom Priest had struck up friendships over the years. Ruud Gullit spent almost the whole game signing autographs before anyone realised that he hadn't been brought on.

The minute he went on the pitch, he played an inch-perfect pass over 40 metres which set up a simple goal. Gullit signed a few more autographs.

The Foes, on the other hand, included various players from teams who had given United a hard time over the years. Stuart Pearce from Nottingham Forest was their captain. He ran on to the field in the Foes' all-black strip with the name 'PSYCHO' written on the back above the number (it was auctioned off for charity after the game). Dave Beasant wore an eye-patch and a stuffed parrot on his shoulder. Gary Lineker went on as a substitute wearing a 'No More Mr Nice Guy' T-shirt and throwing crisps into the crowd. The villainous nature of the Foes side was finally confirmed when Wolf from *Gladiators* ran on for the second half, tripping the referee before the game had even restarted.

In between there was some football, but it was all good knockabout fun. Naturally, the Foes played dirty while the Friends were the heroes. Priest scored two himself and set Les Ferdinand up for a third. Vinnie Jones gave away a penalty which Oldcester's Dutch star, van Brost, put away. Stuart Pearce was the only one who forgot his 'lines', smacking in a 30-yard free kick as if it was the last minute of a vital League game. There were plenty who said it was better than any goal scored at Star Park all season.

Along with about 8,000 others, Nicky howled with laughter all the way through. Chris, on the other hand, missed nearly everything, and by the time the match was over he had already forgotten those parts of the game he had watched with any interest.

Some strange ideas were brewing in his mind. He wasn't sure he understood any of them.

Eight

⚽

After the game, Nicky was all for going straight back to his place to try out the new computer game, but Chris knew he had to be elsewhere. As they crossed the bridge back towards the centre of town, he smacked his head with his palm as if he'd just remembered something.

'Damn! Sorry, Nicky, I've got to meet Rory. I almost forgot!'

'What for?' asked Nicky, with an offended pout on his face. Rory was Chris's strike partner with the Colts. It wasn't that he and Nicky didn't get on, but they had absolutely nothing in common. Chris knew this meant he could rely on Nicky not wanting to tag along.

'I don't know. Something to do with tomorrow's game.' Chris turned quickly to his father. 'I won't be late. I'll get a bus back about six or half past, OK?'

'You'd better,' his dad instructed. 'Dinner at seven, OK?' A casserole was slow-cooking in the oven. Chris knew he'd be grounded for a year if he was late.

'Fine!' said Chris quickly, and he ran off before anyone could say anything else. He had a mental picture of the two of them staring at his retreating back, looking at him as if he was mad.

And maybe he was.

His first stop was a large but tatty record shop on the fringes of Fair Market. Barry's Records was a haphazard, disorganised shambles, but anyone with musical tastes that ran beyond the charts knew they would find what they wanted there.

Chris didn't know anything about rhythm and blues or freeform jazz, but he did know that downstairs in the same department where they sold cassettes, Barry's Records also sold replica football shirts. There wasn't much logic in the arrangement, except that many of Barry's best customers were young men who also liked football. And the shirts did look good, some displayed on the wall, others hanging from racks.

Chris took a long look at the Oldcester shirts, of which (unsurprisingly) there was a big selection. Most dated from the last twenty years, but there were a few of the strip the club had worn in the late sixties. Sometimes, unless the sponsor's name changed, it was hard to tell the difference between them. The red and blue stripes had been a constant. There was even an away shirt from 1977/78 which was all white but had red and blue striped sleeves!

There was nothing, though, quite like the shirt William wore.

'Are you looking for something for yourself, son?' a friendly voice enquired.

It was Barry himself, a round man with white hair and a pale face, who wore a crisp white shirt. The overall effect was to make him look like a ghost, or maybe Jerry after he dipped himself in white paint to fool Tom . . .

'Sort of . . .'

'It's just that there aren't many small sizes,' the shop owner continued, pointing to one end of the rack where a few junior shirts were stored. 'They're a bit pricey, you see. And you lads always want this year's shirt.' He had obviously noted that Chris was wearing his United scarf and had the game's programme peeking out of the pocket of his bomber jacket. 'Been to the game today?'

Chris nodded, then continued briskly, 'Have you got any older shirts?'

Barry looked surprised at that idea. 'When were you thinking of, mate? The fifties?'

'Earlier . . .' replied Chris, uncertain.

'Earlier?' echoed Barry, now amazed. 'You'll be lucky. I see shirts from before the war maybe once a year. They cost hundreds of pounds.'

Chris bit his lip. 'And before that? Before the First World War?'

Barry's bemused smile faded. 'Are you trying to take the Michael, son? You think they made replica shirts back in them

47

days? Seen lots of pictures of kids wearing them in the park, have you? Listen, if a shirt like that was ever found, they'd put it in a museum. It would belong at Star Park, not at the bottom of some kid's wardrobe.'

Chris tried to make some kind of apology. Barry walked away and set about closing up the shop. Chris left in a hurry.

Five minutes later, he was on the bus, heading away from the city centre. It crept through the congested roads leading south from Fair Market, then wound its way south-west through residential districts. Chris watched carefully, keeping an eye out for familiar landmarks. He didn't come to this part of the city very often.

He saw the sign for Rory's road after the bus had passed it, and had to run back from the next stop. He checked his watch – twenty-five past five. Time was getting tight. He found the house OK, but there was a long delay before Mrs Blackstone came to the door. She didn't recognise him.

'I'm afraid Rory's not in,' she said after Chris had explained who he was. 'He's gone to a friend's house.'

'Oh!' Chris fidgeted awkwardly on the doorstep. That put a small dent in his plans.

'Was it something important?' she asked, still wiping her hands on a teacloth.

'I just wanted to borrow Rory's camera,' Chris told her. 'There's something I need to prove to a friend of mine . . .'

Mrs Blackstone caught on quickly that this was going to be a complicated explanation only of interest to young men. She wiped an imaginary smear from the glass of the front door.

'I'm sure it'll be all right,' she said, which caught Chris a little off-balance. 'You can give it back to Rory tomorrow.'

'I could bring it back tonight, if you'd prefer,' Chris replied. 'I don't have to go far.'

'Tomorrow will be fine,' said Mrs Blackstone, and she retreated into the house. Chris spent the subsequent minutes checking his watch every twenty seconds. At last, Mrs Blackstone reappeared dangling Rory's Polaroid camera by its carry-cord.

'I've just remembered!' she said, in her bright voice with its full-on Irish accent. 'You're the boy that plays football with

Rory. I saw you at that game at Easter, when those Americans were over.'

'That's right,' said Chris, his eyes fixed on the camera.

Mrs Blackstone folded her arms, still clutching the camera in her hand. 'That Yank we had staying here had an appetite on him, I can tell you. Were all the Americans like that, do you think? I suppose that's why they're all so fat. I mean, you see Americans on the TV, and they're always fat, don't you think?'

'Yes –' said Chris, squeezing the word into the rapid torrent of Mrs Blackstone's spoken thoughts.

'Of course, we didn't have half the excitement with our young man as you did with yours. Gangsters and FBI men; kidnapping! Lord, your face was in all the papers! To think, we only agreed to Rory playing for your man's team to keep him out of trouble!'

Chris offered a sheepish, desperate smile.

Mrs Blackstone was still in full flow. 'Now Rory says you might become even more famous! He says you've got a trial for the United team, same as he has. Of course, Rory doesn't think he'll make it. What do you think? Is it right what he told me, that if you get through this trial you'll be going to a new school just for football players?'

'Yes –' Chris answered (unable to remember if there had been more than one question in all that). This time he tried to get a 'I'm terribly sorry, but I'm in a hurry – could I take the camera?' into the space between Mrs Blackstone's surging conversation, but he didn't get any further than the 'I'm' before she was continuing, staring out into the garden with a dreamy look on her face.

'I'm sure it's a fine idea. You see some of these professional footballers on the television and they can't string a sentence together. Even our Jack wasn't well spoken, was he, although he was a brilliant manager and a wonderful man.' Chris sighed, wondering how much beyond the one-time Irish manager the conversation would drag. Without thinking, he looked at his watch.

'Are you in a hurry, Chris?' asked Mrs Blackstone. Chris realised that appearances were very deceptive with Mrs Blackstone. She didn't miss a trick.

'I'm sorry, I didn't mean to be rude –' he began.

49

'Never mind. You should have said! I know what it's like with you young men; always in a hurry! Sometimes, I have to say to Rory –'

She caught herself just before she fell over into this new conversational theme. Smiling broadly, she held out the hand with the camera. 'There you go. Sorry about that.'

'I just have to be somewhere in the next half hour,' said Chris as he took the camera.

'Off you go, then. Don't be late.'

Chris started to turn back from the door, but Mrs Blackstone couldn't let him leave without offering one last comment.

'Rory will miss you, if you end up leaving the Colts and he stays behind. He talks about you a lot.' He did? Chris had never thought of Rory as being a particularly close friend, but as he watched a sad shadow creep into Mrs Blackstone's expression, he knew it was true. 'Even so, I know he wants you to do well in the trials. Good luck, Chris.'

The door closed and Chris was left stuck on the Black-stones' front path, feeling awkward and guilty and more confused than ever. It took him almost a minute to tear himself away and start running for his final destination.

'Hey, hey!' yelled the park keeper as Chris tore past. 'We're closing in five minutes!' Chris didn't even break stride. He went through the gates and over towards the gardens, racing across the grass. The park keeper made one more attempt to call him back, but then obviously decided that he was probably just heading for the gates on the far side of the park, taking a short cut home. He was certainly too fast to go chasing after, so the park keeper found some other vital duty he had to take care of.

The park was virtually empty, in stark contrast to the way it had been jammed full of people that morning. Some cloud had drifted over during the afternoon and it had become noticeably cooler. The few people who were left were gradually making their way towards the exits.

Chris ran past the lake and the confectionery stall, cutting over the last patch of grass before the garden. He was breathing hard, having run all the way from Rory's house. It had taken him twenty minutes.

He started to pull up as he closed in on the gate leading into the garden. Even as he reached out for the latch, he could see that it was padlocked.

'Damn!' he whispered under his breath.

He could see one of the gardeners nearby, sweeping up rubbish from the footpath near the shop. Chris ran over to him.

'Excuse me, could you let me into the gardens for just a moment?'

'It's locked,' said the man without looking up. Chris groaned. Those two words had made it clear that the man was one of those 'I've got a uniform so it's my job to say no to everything' types.

'I just need a minute,' Chris pleaded. He held up the camera. 'Just long enough to take a picture of the war memorial. It's for a school project.'

'Come back tomorrow.'

All kinds of good ideas were forming in Chris's mind — excuses, apologies and stories about how he couldn't go back tomorrow and about how the homework was due on Monday. Chris didn't bother with any of them. No matter how inventive he was, how quickly he thought, he knew the jobsworth would have a ready reply, and that reply would always be 'no'.

'Thanks!' said Chris, and he took off again, heading off towards the corner of the garden. He knew instinctively that this would cause the gardener to abandon his fascinating and crucial sweeping duties, so that he could watch to make sure Chris didn't have any ideas of climbing the fence.

Which, of course, he did.

Chris gave the man as little time as he could to react. The moment he was out of sight round the corner, he grabbed hold of a tree branch that was stretched out over the fence, used his other hand to steady himself on the top, then vaulted over.

In fact, he acted so quickly he didn't even have time to ask himself what he was doing.

William wouldn't be there, of course. That wasn't what he was expecting to find. That wouldn't make sense.

Chris pushed through the undergrowth, trying to take out some insurance against being caught by not actually killing anything. Moments later, he was in the space around the fountain. Everything was calm and peaceful, almost silent save for the rustling of the trees and the constant background birdsong. There was no sign of any of the park staff.

He aimed for the memorial, moving as quickly as he dared, sure that he'd be caught.

But no, he was OK. In the dark shadow around the statue he could start to relax. He came to a halt, looking up at the sad-faced warrior on the plinth, forever looking back for his friends, knowing that they could never come. Was he meant to be the sole survivor, Chris wondered?

Picking up some newspaper from the rubbish scattered around the base, he quickly rubbed at the stone plinth. The dirt came away grudgingly. Chris cleaned off what he could in a few minutes, revealing most of the names. His eyes scanned them all as he worked. It felt quite strange, revealing their identities after . . . well, who knew how long they had been obscured? All these long-dead names. There was no-one here to put faces to them; no-one who could tell any stories about them. But they were men from Oldcester, and their families might well still live in the city or the surrounding towns. Perhaps some memories of them lingered on.

The thought sent a chill up Chris's spine. The evening sun must have tucked behind a cloud, he thought, sensing the shadows darkening around him. Even the birds had stopped singing.

He stepped back, aimed the Polaroid at the plinth and took a picture of the names carved there. The camera whirred as it fed the print out through the slot at the bottom. Chris remained still, waiting for it to develop.

'Hello again.'

The voice caught him so much by surprise he almost dropped the camera as he spun round. Juggling it precariously in his hands, he caught sight of William watching him with an amused smile on his face. Chris finally got his fingers locked around the cord, and the camera was safe.

'Perhaps you should think of playing in goal,' William observed.

'They'd have to put a string on the ball first,' Chris replied, showing how he'd managed to catch the camera. William smiled, then looked past him at the statue. His eyes seemed to glaze over for a moment, then he looked down at Chris once again.

'I'm glad you could make it,' he said.

'I'm sorry?' said Chris, off-balance once again. His mind was racing to keep up.

'I wasn't sure you'd come.'

It slowly dawned on Chris what William was talking about. 'Our arrangement is for tomorrow . . .' he said.

William's face registered understanding and disappointment in close succession. 'What day is it today?' he asked.

'Saturday,' replied Chris.

William nodded, and drew in a deep breath. 'Of course, we agreed Sunday, didn't we? After your game.' He scratched at his brow, reflecting on the mistake (or at least that's how it seemed to Chris).

'Still, now you're here . . .'

'It's late,' said Chris quickly, and he was surprised to find that he was actually afraid, though he had no idea what of. 'I don't have my ball here . . . and the park's closing now.' He gestured at his watch. 'If we don't get out of here now, we'll be locked in.'

William nodded in agreement. Chris walked past him, away from the statue. After he had taken a few more steps, he paused and looked back. William didn't appear to be following.

'Aren't you coming?' he asked.

'I have something to do,' William replied vaguely. 'I should have taken care of it earlier, but I lost track of time.'

Chris started to offer a comment, but decided against it.

'I'd better be going,' he said.

'I'll see you tomorrow,' said William, smiling.

Chris nodded, and stepped further away before stopping again. William was watching him.

'William, I was wondering . . . where did you get that shirt?'

William looked down at his breast, taking the bottom of the jersey between his fingers and lifting it away from his belly, as if he needed to see just what it was he was wearing.

53

'It was given to me . . .' he said. There was no mistaking the emotion in his voice as he spoke. His pride was evident, etched deep in his face. Chris knew that feeling. The first time he had pulled on Spirebrook Comp's kit; the first time he had turned out for the Colts. That was a moment you never forgot. One day, Chris wanted to feel the same way about an Oldcester United shirt.

'William . . .' Chris began, intending to ask him about when he'd played, but the young man had already turned away, as if he was going to step around the statue. 'William!' Chris called, with a little more urgency. William looked up, and there was a glint of something in his eyes that could have been fear, could have been anger. 'You don't . . . live here . . . do you?'

William laughed. 'No, I live over by Star Park. Warwick Street. The ground is that close, when the sun's low in the winter, it throws shadows across our house.' He looked around. 'I'd better get back there, soon.'

Chris wanted to ask him what he was doing in the park; wanted to ask him what his job was, what his life was like. There were plenty of questions. It was just a case of picking the right one.

While he hesitated, William stepped away. One more stride and he would be gone.

Instinctively, Chris snatched up the camera, aimed it roughly at the statue and clicked the button. The flash disorientated him for a second, it had seemed so bright. When he stopped blinking, William was gone.

The print was ejected from the slot at the front of the camera. Chris took it between thumb and finger, waving it in the air.

While he waited, he threw the camera cord over his shoulder and took a look at the first picture, which had developed clear and sharp. He could read every name, which was a relief because he hadn't been certain it would work.

He waited in the gardens for the second picture to develop. He waited quite a long time. Even after the picture had appeared, he waited a little longer. He had no idea how he got out of the park, nor how he got home, but he was late and the casserole was ruined.

Nine

It wasn't that he was playing badly. He'd scored a tap-in goal in the first half and had nearly set up Jazz for a second. But as he turned away from having hit a volley over the bar, Chris knew his game was just that little bit off. That was all it took. Against a team this good, the Colts needed to be at their best.

Several players on the Wombourne team were being watched by Endsleigh League sides in the West Midlands. There was a fast, well-balanced midfield player named David who was supposed to have caught the eye of Aston Villa. Rumour had it that some of the spectators on the touchlines were scouts. Chris had seen Ray Foulds, the scout who had first seen him at Spirebrook – the man who had introduced him to Sean Priest and the possibility of playing for United.

As Chris ran backwards towards the halfway line, he doubted that many of the other scouts were watching him.

'I must concentrate!' he told himself. As he looked across to Rory, he received a friendly smile and a raised fist from his team mate which, he knew, were meant to encourage him. Clearly, Rory thought Chris wasn't 100 per cent in the game as well.

Chris nodded, and clapped his hands, trying to lift the others.

Three-one down and less than twenty minutes to go. Chris knew that defeat today would mean the end of the season for the Colts. Not that it had been a bad season – winning the district league was a pretty good achievement and the exchange visit with the American students had been brilliant – but there had been a number of disappointments in the

Cup competitions they had entered. Now this one was going the same way.

Wombourne's keeper thumped the goal kick upfield where Mac was beaten in the air by a lad with long hair. A space opened, but the Colts defence shut it down quickly. Zak fed the ball out to Polly, who looked to find Chris moving into space on the right.

Chris's marker was a lively lad, very left-footed, who liked to push forward. He was out of position now. Polly's quick pass could have set Chris free on the wing, able to cut inside or push to the goal-line to make a telling cross. Instead, to the moans of the crowd, Chris's first touch was a bad one, and the ball spilled across the line into touch.

The shock of having made such a hash of it brought Chris back from his foggy daydream. He saw Polly turn away to hide his anger, but there was no mistaking the way the midfielder smashed one fist into the palm of the other hand. Chris shook his head. In those last few seconds, William had taken Chris's mind off the game again.

Chris was wild with himself, but it was as if part of him really didn't want to be there. He couldn't control the way his mind kept wandering, or the crazy thoughts it latched on to.

A few moments later, there was a break in play when one of the Wombourne defenders took a whack on the back of the head as their keeper tried to fist a cross away. Iain Walsh called Chris over to the touchline.

'They're not looking good at the back,' he counselled. 'Put the pressure on and we could still get this back.'

'OK,' said Chris.

'But you've got to get your head together, Chris. I'm relying on you.'

Chris nodded. He had expected the Colts' manager to realise that something was wrong – Walsh had too good an eye and he knew his players well. On several Sundays during the season, Walsh led the Colts in the morning game even though he had an important match himself that afternoon, playing for Riverside's first eleven. He never allowed anything to distract him. He demanded nothing less from his players.

'Is this trial getting to you?' he asked.

A week ago he would have been spot on. Now, Chris realised, even the trial wasn't occupying him the way it had.

'Yes, I think it must be,' he said.

'One game at a time,' said Walsh. Chris nodded, relieved that Walsh was in a sympathetic mood. Ordinarily, he was really fierce with players he thought weren't giving 100 per cent. It dawned on Chris that he hadn't really been in Walsh's bad books since the incident with Russell Jones, when Chris had tried to get the new boy kicked off the team and had quit himself when Walsh wouldn't back down. Now, if things turned out as planned, Chris was playing his last game for the Colts anyway, while Russell was firmly in place as their keeper and Chris's friend.

It was strange how things had turned out.

But, Chris thought, not as strange as what he had come to believe about William. Perhaps he could talk to Walsh about it, explain what was on his mind. Perhaps he could . . .

Chris realised Walsh was staring at him. He knew he had drifted off again.

'Whatever it is, Chris, get it together.'

'I'll try,' Chris replied.

The game restarted. A minute or so later, the Colts won a free kick. Jazz lined up to take it.

Chris hung back outside the box, trying to avoid drawing much attention to himself. In the middle, Rory was a visible nuisance and the keeper and his central defenders were fussing around him like tugs round a supertanker. Zak made things worse by walking solidly through their ranks to take up position on the near post.

Jazz raised his hand. At the same moment, Tollie ran an overlap outside him which drew all the defenders half a pace to their right. Chris started his run, ghosting in from the corner of the penalty area, aiming for clear space just in front of the far post.

Jazz hit the cross perfectly. The keeper froze on his line, and the defenders turned as they saw the ball being hit across them. Chris started to gather himself to jump.

In that same instant, from the corner of his eye, Chris saw someone walking across the grass past the ruins of the old changing rooms. The bright red and blue of his United shirt was lit up by a shaft of sunlight.

The ball brought Chris's attention back to the present with a solid whack. He had been in the process of drawing his head back to strike when his eyes flicked away. Jazz's quick cross was travelling fast, and as it smacked into Chris's brow, it flipped his whole body back so far that his feet flew into the air.

Chris's attention was firmly on the game now. He waited for the impact.

Knowing that he was going to arrive at ground level hard, Chris instinctively dropped his hands to cushion the blow. His left hand skidded away across the turf, his right jammed and twisted. A micro-second later, his body hit the floor with bone-jarring force.

He lay there for a moment, aware only of the clouds skidding across the sky above him, then everything went dark.

Fortunately, the blackness was caused only by the crowding round of the other players. Chris knew what it was like to black out, and he wasn't eager to experience it again.

Of course, unconsciousness had some advantages. Like he wouldn't be able to feel the searing pain in his right elbow or the dull ache around his back.

Iain Walsh arrived moments later, with Sean Priest immediately behind him. He often popped up late to see how the Colts had fared in their morning games. It was a standing joke that he arrived at the last moment deliberately, just so he could see how late Chris would leave it to score the winner.

He usually wore either a suit or some well-coordinated casual clothes and a leather jacket. Priest liked to be well dressed. Today, he was wearing old jeans, and had left his jacket behind to enjoy the sunshine in a short-sleeved United shirt.

'Are you hurting anywhere?' asked Walsh, looking Chris in the eyes.

'Just my pride,' confessed Chris, trying to shut out the stabbing sensation on the outside of his right arm.

'Did you hit your head?'

'After getting clocked by the ball?' Chris asked. 'No . . . honestly, I'm OK.'

After another minute the Colts' manager helped his striker to his feet. Everyone saw how Chris winced as he came upright.

'I've banged my arm a little,' Chris admitted. He hobbled round a little, stiff and sore all over, but mostly focusing on the sharp pain his arm was causing him. If he moved it, it was really painful.

'I'll tell Marsh to get ready,' said Priest, reading Walsh's mind. Chris thought about protesting, but then closed his mouth and allowed himself to be steered off the pitch behind the goal.

Walsh was no doctor, but he had enough training to decide that the fall had caused no more than a few bruises. Once back at the side of the pitch, though, when he asked Chris to try and stretch out his arm, it was clear that Chris was having difficulty fighting back the tears as he did so.

'Could be the ligaments, or maybe you've torn the triceps tendon,' Walsh announced. 'Either way, I think we ought to get a doctor to look at it.' Chris heard Priest and Walsh talk about who would run Chris to the hospital.

'Not casualty, please . . .' sighed Chris, trying to make light of the injury. 'I'll go and see the doctor . . . he only lives a few doors up from us.'

The two men looked at each other.

'Come on,' Chris continued, trying to sound bright about it. 'You know what casualty will be like on a Sunday. I'll still be there on Tuesday.'

He finally talked them round. Priest said he'd drive Chris home. As they pulled away from the makeshift cinder car park, the referee was blowing his whistle on the Colts' season. While the others were shaking hands and wondering what they'd do with their Sundays over the summer, Chris went off, perhaps leaving it all behind for ever.

Ten

⚽

Dr Loenikov was a Ukrainian, who talked all the time about going back to his homeland 'now that it is free of Russian rule', but who had lived in England for so long that he had a broad Midlands accent and a taste for golf and strong beer. He was about three years short of retirement, and not one of his patients expected him to move any further away from Spirebrook than a cottage overlooking the golf course on the Derby Road.

He'd been the Stephens' family GP for longer than Chris had been alive, and he made a point of keeping up to date with Chris's progress. In the last few years, mercifully, conversation had switched from what a noisy baby Chris had been to how his football career was shaping up. When Mr Stephens walked Chris down the road that afternoon, Dr Loenikov was more than happy to open the surgery and take a look at the injury.

Like all GPs, Dr Loenikov was a follower of the 'does this hurt?' school of doctoring. Chris was sure that he believed that the louder a patient yelled, the worse the problem must be (although there had to be a point when that didn't work any more; he couldn't imagine doctors believed some poor bloke in a coma was OK just because he didn't scream when he prodded him).

Chris gritted his teeth as Dr Loenikov held up his arm and asked him to straighten the elbow. A small whimper escaped between his lips.

'I don't think it's too bad,' the doctor explained to Mr Stephens. 'Probably just a strain; maybe a small tear. Just don't try playing cricket or picking your nose with it and you'll be fine.'

'How long will it take to heal?' asked Chris's father.

Dr Loenikov knew about the trial. 'He'll be OK next weekend, I think. I'll prescribe some pain-killers for now and we'll look again on Tuesday.' He turned to Chris. 'You could maybe wear a sling for a few days . . .'

He was impressed when Chris agreed to whatever suggestions he had to make. 'You boys, you normally try to be so macho about these things.'

Mr Stephens helped Chris step down from the couch and threw his jacket on across his shoulders.

'I appreciate this, Dr Loenikov. I didn't mean to interrupt your Sunday lunch.'

'No problem,' the GP replied, turning round with a small plastic tub of the pain-killers. 'Call round anytime. Next time, though, forget about the injury thing first. We could just go to the pub for lunch, OK?'

'Sure.' Chris's father grinned gratefully. 'We'll do that.'

'Now, listen,' Dr Loenikov advised. 'These tablets, you take three a day, and maybe one more if the pain is acute at any time, OK? They may make you feel a bit woozy, so no tightrope walking. Oh, and you may have some very strange dreams for a night or two. Don't worry about it.'

Chris almost mentioned that he had been having some pretty good dreams while he was awake, but he decided against it. Dr Loenikov was off on a new subject.

'Looking forward to next season? It'll be good to have United back in the Premiership again.'

He guided them back through his house and out the front door.

'Hey, Chris,' he said as they walked down the path. 'Don't forget, come back on Tuesday if you have any pain. But if I don't see you, good luck next weekend.'

'Thank you,' said Chris. He felt a lot better now that he knew no serious damage had been done.

At the doctor's front gate, Mr Stephens turned automatically for home. It took him a moment to realise that Chris wasn't alongside him.

'Where do you think you're going?' he asked, once he'd turned round to find his son nervously hesitating, neither following nor going away. Chris noted the words. *Where do you think you're going?* not *Where are you going?* That implied that Chris's father had already decided the answer to the second question.

'I said I'd see Nicky . . .'

'Forget it. You're coming home. We're having Sunday dinner in an hour and a half. You're spending the time resting.'

'But this was arranged . . .'

'Unarrange it. Tell Nicky he can come round to us.'

Chris could feel that his father wasn't going to give in. He made one last attempt to break the deadlock.

'We said we'd meet someone . . .'

'Forget it! Didn't I ground you last night after you didn't come home for dinner?'

'No, you didn't!'

'Well, I can change my mind. Or I can ground you for something else. There's bound to be something. There always is with you.'

That struck Chris as being a trifle unfair. He wasn't a troublemaker or anything like that. He kept his room neat, he studied hard and he didn't have any friends who left stains on the carpet. Apart from a few run-ins with Mrs Cole at school and the odd adventure with international criminals, he led a very quiet life.

'As soon as I saw Sean Priest bring you home, I knew something was up. Every time I see that man, something bad has happened.'

That was a little unfair too. Clearly Chris's father didn't care who he offended today. Perhaps all the tension that Chris had been feeling about the trial had transferred to him.

'It's just a routine knock,' Chris tried to explain. 'Could have happened any time.'

'But it's happened today. And you have just five days to shake it off before the trial. I know how important that is to you, and I know how miserable you'll be if you fail because of an injury. So, for the next five days you're going to rest that arm if I have to glue it to your bed.'

End of discussion.

As soon as they got indoors, Chris rang Nicky and asked him to come round. He told his best friend about the accident. Nicky, probably hoping to see blood all over the place, agreed to set off as soon as he'd finished dinner. Having eaten one of Mrs Fiorentini's meals, Chris knew that could mean Nicky arriving in 30 minutes or in five hours. He urged his friend to hurry.

Shortly afterwards, Chris's father called for him to wash for lunch.

'How am I supposed to do that with my arm glued to the bed?' quipped Chris.

If that was supposed to put his father in a better mood, it failed completely.

Nicky almost had trouble getting up the stairs. A few extra Fiorentinis had arrived for dinner, so Nicky's mum had sacrificed an entire supermarket's stock to the feast. Nicky was stuffed to the eyebrows.

He and Chris sat up in Chris's bedroom. Nicky propped himself against the wall in a way that suggested he might nod off at any minute. Chris decided to give him the facts quickly.

'I saw William again,' said Chris.

Nicky managed to appear interested. 'When?'

'Last night. When I left you after the match, I went to see if I could find out some more about him.'

'How?'

'Well, I thought that if you were right about him living rough in the park, I'd find him there at closing time with whatever he used to sleep in. First, though, I went to Barry's Records.'

'Why?' asked Nicky, yawning. Chris couldn't see any way Nicky could get around to Where? or Who?, so he hoped that his friend would start to play a more active role in the conversation soon.

'I wanted to check out that business about the shirt. You know, I said William had a replica United shirt?'

'Yeah, I remember. So what? There are plenty of them about. We've both got one.'

Chris wasn't so sure it was going to help having Nicky join in after all, if that was going to be the level of his assistance.

'It's an old one, Nicky – remember? Anyway, while we were in the museum . . .'

'Who?'

So, he'd managed it after all. 'You and me! Yesterday, remember?'

Nicky looked confused. 'Stop dodging about!' he insisted. 'I thought you were talking about Barry's Records!'

Chris had to accept that he wasn't presenting the information in the most logical way. He decided to reveal the story in the order it had happened, starting with the 1905 picture in the museum, his brief conversation about replica shirts with Barry, borrowing Rory's camera (which he had safely returned) and then meeting William in the park.

'You went to take a picture of the memorial?'

'Yes,' said Chris.

'Why?'

You've used that one, Chris thought to himself. He took a moment to regroup, then prepared to lead Nicky towards the only solution that made sense.

'Look, just follow this through, will you?' He gave Nicky a pad of A4 and a pen. Nicky liked to make notes when they were engaged on working out a puzzle like this.

'William says he played for United, right? He's no more than twenty-five so he had to have played in the 1980s or 1990s. We've never heard of him, and we're pretty sure his name wasn't on any of the lists in the museum.'

'Which means he's either lying or he just meant the Second Eleven or something.'

'Maybe,' said Chris, who wasn't ready to let Nicky have a glimpse of the third option just yet. He kept going, counting on his fingers as he ticked off the points (which was usually Nicky's job in these circumstances as well). 'He hangs around the war memorial at the park. That's twice I've seen him there. He wears a replica United shirt, the same style as I saw in a photo from 1905. He told me it was given to him. But when I asked in Barry's Records about shirts that were that old, I was told you couldn't get them for love nor money.'

'Perhaps it's a copy,' said Nicky, which immediately threw Chris out of his stride. It didn't help that Chris had reached point five in his counting and was wondering if he dared lift his injured arm a little to continue on his other hand. 'Perhaps his mum makes clothes, and copied the old shirt for him,' Nicky said, developing his idea. He had doodled a swirling pattern on the pad. 'I don't know where you're going with this, Chris. Why were you taking pictures of the war memorial? What was that supposed to prove?'

Chris decided it was time to cut to the chase.

'It was supposed to help me track him down. I wanted to get all the names and that was the quick way to do it. You see, I think William's name is on there.' He took a deep breath, and went for it. 'I think William is a ghost.'

They argued about the facts for another hour, by which time it was nearly four o'clock. Chris tried to wrap up the discussion, since he had a favour to ask Nicky and time was pressing.

'Look at the photographs again!' he insisted.

The good thing about the way the discussion was working out was that he had Nicky's full attention. Three pages of the A4 pad were filled with Nicky's spidery handwriting, with headings, facts and conclusions all over the place, many of them crossed out.

Nicky picked up the first Polaroid. It showed the names of about 40 soldiers and sailors, by rank, initial and surname. Chris had explained that the photo showed just one patch of the plinth. There were five Ws among the initials.

'What do you think that proves?' Nicky insisted.

'William's an old name, Nicky. How many Williams do you know?'

'Isn't there a Prince William?' his friend asked. That threw them both for a moment – neither could be called a close follower of royal events. Nicky threw out a few more names, including Willy Carson, William Shatner and William Tell.

'OK, OK,' Chris said, holding up one hand to quell Nicky's growing list. 'Why does William – our William – hang around the war memorial?'

'I gave you a reason for that on Saturday,' Nicky insisted. 'I bet there's a residential care home near there. Or maybe he really is sleeping rough in the gardens somewhere.'

'What, and he goes home to his mum for dinner and clean football shirts?'

Nicky wasn't interested in that line of argument. 'Just because I can't say for sure what he is, doesn't mean he's a ghost!'

Which was true. Chris started to realise just how hard it was to make a complete case for anything about William. Did the police always have this problem, dealing with half-facts and conclusions?

'OK. The second photo.'

Nicky sighed, not even bothering to pick it up.

'Chris, it doesn't show anything. Just the side of the statue. A bit wonky, too.'

'My point exactly! Where is William?'

'What do you mean, where is he? You must have missed him, you dope. He'd gone off into the trees, or behind the memorial.'

'He was there! I saw him! And look, don't you think that's a shadow, there on the bush? Where's that coming from?'

Nicky tutted, but he did at least take another look at the Polaroid.

'Chris, it's a fuzzy picture of nothing. If that is a shadow, it could have been made by the statue itself.'

Chris tried once again to make a point about the direction the sun was coming from and how the statue was too high to make the shadow but it was hopeless. In the end, all he had was his own certain memory. William had been standing in front of that bush when he took the picture.

He was sure of that. Wasn't he?

'Go back to Saturday, then,' he said. 'What was going on there? One minute I've got the ball, the next minute I haven't. I played heading tennis with William, but according to those kids I left the ball outside the garden.'

Nicky clearly had no idea what Chris was trying to say. In truth, Chris wasn't that sure either. He had this strong sense that something had been strange and unreal about the encounter, but the facts themselves were as transparent as ghosts were supposed to be.

'Chris, you know as well as I do that you were dehydrated that morning . . .'

'How could I have been? All I did was catch the bus to the park.'

'You drank a can and a half in about thirty seconds as soon as I saw you –'

'So what are you saying? I dreamt the whole thing? Left the ball outside and –'

'No, I'm not saying anything for certain. All I'm saying is you could have left the ball outside –'

'And wandered round the garden talking to myself and playing football with a ghost and an imaginary ball –'

'Or you could have had the ball, but lost it. Maybe that kid you saw first took it. Maybe the kids we caught playing with it found it inside the garden.'

'But you don't know, do you?'

'The thing is, we just don't know!'

These last two sentences came out simultaneously, at the end of a fast exchange of opinions in which Chris had interrupted Nicky and Nicky had interrupted Chris. They'd achieved as much in that one conversation as they had in the hour before.

'You have to admit it's all a bit weird,' Chris said at last, once they had both calmed down.

'Sure,' said Nicky, grudgingly. 'But weird doesn't mean ghost. I just think you're a bit tense because of the trial.'

Chris leaned back on the chair in front of his desk as if Nicky had just produced the clinching argument – in his favour.

'That's the strangest thing of all, Nicky. Since I first met William, I haven't been thinking about the trial at all. Before, yeah, it was the only thing on my mind. My stomach's been in a knot for weeks! But now, it's like the trial isn't even happening. I'm distracted by the least thing, but not because of what might happen next weekend.'

Nicky could see that Chris was telling the truth. It was rare for Nicky to suffer any kind of anxiety at all, and he was still pretty calm about the big event. However, he knew Chris was different.

'OK . . .' he started and he picked up the pen. 'Let's say there is something odd about everything that's happened. Let's even say that it would be worth digging around a bit, just to find out who this William guy is . . .'

Chris smiled broadly. Nicky was on his side.

'Yeah? What should we do, then?'

'Well, we should hunt around for some more facts, find out more about him.' Nicky picked up the pad and turned to a fresh page. 'We need to find out if anyone called William has ever played for Oldcester, even right back in the past. I bet the museum has records . . .'

'Last time I saw him, he said he lived in Warwick Street, somewhere near Star Park. We could check that out . . .'

'Great!' agreed Nicky, adding this to the new list. 'Of course, what would really help is if we could see him again – ask him his surname, stuff like that.'

Now Chris was smiling so wide it looked as if his face might split.

'Actually, Nicky, I've been meaning to talk to you about that.'

Eleven

Chris and Nicky barely speaking wasn't something new. Most of their mutual friends had lived through their periodic squabbles. Along the way, they had learned that the best thing to do was keep a low profile. These things blew over pretty quickly.

Most arguments between Chris and Nicky centred over some trivial detail about football matches, TV shows (there had been a long feud over whether Sheridan was a better commander on *Babylon 5* than Sinclair) and school. Nicky was impulsive, and prone to lose track of things after a while, which meant sometimes he took both sides in an argument. Chris was more determined and straight-dealing.

In the end, their friendship counted for more than anything they ever argued about. Knowing that, whenever they were arguing, everyone around them stepped back and waited for peace negotiations to start.

Monday morning, before school, things were different. There was actually quite a crowd around Chris and Nicky, paying close attention to everything that was said. Some were even taking part, after a fashion.

'So . . . is he invisible, then?' asked Fuller.

'He must be!' Nicky snapped grumpily. 'I spent an hour and a half in the park waiting for him to show, but he never did.'

Griff and Fuller chuckled behind their hands, delighted to hear that Nicky had been sent off on a wild goose chase. Even when Griff was captain of the school team, he and Nicky had banged heads all the time. Fuller just liked to see things go wrong for other people.

'So, there was no ghost, then?' asked Jazz, who was taking the story much more seriously than the older boys.

'Of course not!' snapped Nicky. 'There never was! And this William bloke is just a time-waster.'

Chris decided to repeat the apology he had made ten times that morning already. 'He said he'd be there . . .' he began.

Nicky made a dismissive, snorting sound. 'Yeah, yeah. Maybe he just forgot! Maybe things were busy in heaven and he couldn't keep track of time.' He glowered at some of the audience who were giggling. 'Or maybe this was your idea of a wind-up, Chris?'

'What do you mean?'

'Well, you're the only one to have seen this William bloke. Maybe it was a joke — your joke — all along.'

Looking around, Chris saw that several of the others were prepared to believe that too. And they'd admire him for it.

'Look, Nicky, I said I'm sorry and I meant it. William said he'd meet me in the park yesterday, and I thought he'd be there. You know why I couldn't go myself.' He motioned with his head towards his arm, which was safely tucked inside the sling. 'I honestly didn't mean to yank your chain.'

Nicky wasn't even partially convinced, and made an exaggerated version of the snorting noise to show it. Chris became aware that more and more people were being attracted to their huddle, wondering what was going on. He wondered if he could convince Nicky to continue this conversation later on.

There was little chance of that.

'Do you really think William is a ghost, then?' asked Jazz. Mac pressed closer too. From what Chris knew of Mac's chosen reading matter, he was sure Mac was more certain of the existence of the paranormal than Fox Mulder.

'I'm not sure,' he replied, trying to hedge his bets. Nicky didn't allow him to escape so lightly.

'Oh, right. So what was all that round at your place yesterday afternoon? You were sure about ghosts then!' He turned his face to look around the crowd. 'He's got a photograph to prove it! It's a picture with no-one in it, so it has to be a picture of a ghost. Then there's the fact that someone whose name begins with a 'W' died in the First World War . . . well, what can I say?'

70

Nicky was managing to make Chris's evidence sound very stupid, even to Chris's ears. Perhaps he had managed to get the whole thing out of shape.

'Ghosts don't show up on photographs,' announced Mac. 'Not unless you see their aura.'

Nicky threw his hands up in the air. 'Don't you start!' he moaned.

'There are plenty of pictures like the one that Chris took. Sometimes, all you can see is a kind of outline of light . . . other times there's a vague, misty suggestion of someone in the picture.' Mac's eyes closed, as if he was imagining just such a photo. 'And sometimes, like in Chris's picture, there's evidence that someone is there – like a shadow – but no sign of the actual person.'

Nicky muttered something to the effect that Mac wouldn't show up on a picture either, seeing as he wasn't all there, but the group was much more interested in what Mac had to say. Realising that he had an audience, Mac scratched his head and launched off into a personal story.

'About three years ago, my uncle – who lives in Canada – used up a whole roll of film when he and some ex-army buddies went away fishing for the weekend. When he got back home, he learned that my grandmother – his mum – had died back here in England. He flew over for the funeral.

'While he was over here, he helped my father go through all gran's stuff. One of the things they noticed was that there were no pictures of her from before they were born. They both said what a pity that was, because it would have been nice to have a record of her whole life. But they didn't find anything belonging to gran that was older than about forty years or so.

'With the funeral and everything over, my uncle went back to America. Once he got home, he remembered the film he had taken and sent it to be developed. Two days later, he picked it up.

'There was one frame on the picture that Uncle Lewis didn't expect to have come out. It had been late in the evening and the flash gun hadn't fired. So, when he got the film back he was surprised to find that all twenty-four frames had come out. And right in the middle of the film, the tenth picture he'd taken, was this young woman in a long coat, standing outside their old house in front of a really old-looking car. She was really pretty, just like people always said about my gran, and some experts have looked at the picture and said that from the clothes and the car and stuff, the picture would have to date from about 1945, when my gran would have been about eighteen.'

Mac sat back on the bench, his story completed. Some of the crowd that had been listening swapped looks or whispered 'Wow!' under their breath. A few laughed it off, but the majority were convinced it was true.

Nicky, of course, remained among the doubters. 'So? What does that prove? It doesn't have to have been a picture of your nan; it doesn't have to have been her ghost!'

'Think about it, Nicky. My uncle tried to take a picture the moment she died . . .'

Nicky pressed up close to Mac. Although Fiorentini was no giant himself, he was easily taller than Mac, who was a year younger and short even among his classmates. Mac had put up with a lot due to his lack of size, including any number of times when older boys had tried to intimidate him. It never worked. Both on the football pitch and in the rest of his life, Mac made up for the lack of a few centimetres in height by being remarkably big-hearted, which counted for a lot more.

It was almost funny watching Nicky trying to defeat him by looming over him like a giant and shouting. When he'd played in goal for the school and for the Colts, plenty of strikers had tried the same thing with Mac. It didn't work; at least, not every time.

'Or it could have been a foul-up at the processing lab,' Nicky said, looking quite fierce. 'Uncle Fabian once had a whole film come back of farm animals, when he'd been taking pictures at a family birthday party.'

Nicky was distracted from the discussion when Griff asked, 'What's your point?' Griff towered over Nicky to much the same degree that Nicky towered over Mac. It was like watching a CD-Rom of a food chain in action. While Nicky tried to defend his family's honour, Chris was free to move closer to Mac.

'So, you believe in this stuff? Ghosts? The supernatural?' he asked.

Mac nodded, flicking his eyes around quickly to make sure he wasn't in a minority of one. 'There's all kinds of stuff we don't know about, Chris. Who's to say that when you die your spirit can't stay bound to the earth? Maybe this William guy left something unresolved when he died, something he hadn't done. Maybe he's got to sort it out before his soul can be free.'

Nicky was back. Apparently family honour wasn't that important.

'So where's he been up to now, eh? Chris saw him, what, Saturday, for the first time? If he died all that time ago, where's he been up to now?'

Mac didn't have any answers. Nicky took the small mid-fielder's silence to be proof that his argument had won, raising his eyebrows at Chris as if to ask if he'd had enough.

'Maybe something's brought him back,' said Chris.

Nicky almost shrieked with rage. 'Let it go!' he demanded.

Chris shrank back a little in the face of Nicky's fury, but his mind was made up.

'The only way to settle this is to find out more about William,' he insisted. 'I mean, it ought to be easy enough to find out if he's a real person.'

Mac nodded, and Chris got the idea that he could count on at least one person to help in the quest. Russell and Jazz were hanging around in a way that suggested they might be prepared to get involved, so long as they didn't have to do anything too weird.

Instinctively, though, Chris looked again at Nicky.

He just couldn't imagine continuing to explore the William mystery without his best friend, the guy who had — after all — been part of (and cause of!) nearly all of the best adventures of his life. Surely Nicky would want to go along with the game; to expose William as nothing but an ordinary bloke, if nothing else?

Nicky could feel their eyes on him, and knew what it meant. 'You have to be kidding!' he laughed, taking a step back. 'I've done my time! Ninety minutes in a park! If you guys want to waste time chasing after ghosts, that's fine. Not me. No way.'

73

The bell rang to announce the start of the last-but-one day of term.

'Suit yourself,' sighed Chris. He turned to the others. 'Let's meet up at break and decide what we do next.'

The other three agreed that this would make sense, then they all stood up, fastening their jackets and hoisting their bags as they prepared to make their way into class. The rest of the crowd drifted away ahead of them. Chris was biting his lip as he saw Nicky hanging back, keeping within earshot.

As they set off towards the main doors, Nicky piped up from the rear of the group. 'Wouldn't lunchtime be better?' No-one answered, although all four of them allowed small smiles to creep on to their faces. 'Did you hear what I said?' Nicky continued, a little more forcefully. 'Lunchtime would be better . . . we'd have more time. We'll have to work out who's going to follow up which lead.'

The others were all grinning, trying to keep their heads straight as they entered the passage leading to the class-rooms. Not one of them wanted Nicky to see their faces.

'This had better not be a wind-up,' they heard him mutter, by which time none of them could have kept a straight face if they tried.

Twelve

Following the action plan Nicky had drawn up at lunchtime, they split up into three groups after school, each with their own job to do.

Mac and Russell set off for Memorial Park, to find out if William was there, to see if there was any way he had been living rough inside the park, and to look for hostels, cheap hotels or other places he might have been staying in.

Jazz agreed to see what he could find in the central library. This suited him best, since he could hardly explain to his father that he wanted to go skulking round the streets with the likes of Chris Stephens, who seemed to have had his picture in the papers more often than the bloke who did the horoscopes.

Chris and Nicky, meanwhile, were going to Star Park, to see if they could find out if anyone called William had ever played football for United.

They would compare notes that night.

Nicky was in quite a bright mood during the afternoon. The day's lessons had all been pretty laid back, and Nicky had scored the winning goal in the lunchtime game, nutmegging Fuller on the way to scoring. They sat on the upper deck of the bus into town, chattering about the day's events, and making plans for the summer holidays. They avoided the G-word carefully. Chris didn't want another argument . . . at least not until after dinner.

Instead, Nicky managed to steer the conversation round to another subject Chris had been avoiding recently. The trials.

'Will it be the same as last year, do you think?' asked Nicky.

'I guess so,' said Chris, assuming Nicky meant the format, not the outcome. He had no reason to think otherwise.

Nicky digested this opinion slowly, staring out of the

window at the traffic streaming away from the city centre.

'You know, I've thought a lot about last year,' he said after a while. 'And I think I know why it was that we didn't get selected.'

It came as quite a shock to Chris to realise that this was a conversation he and Nicky had never had. At the time of the previous trial, they had both been so uptight about other things that failing to make the cut was the only logical outcome of their efforts. The detailed reasons why didn't seem important.

At least, they hadn't been important to Chris. Clearly, Nicky had given it more consideration.

He was leaning forward on the seat in front, still staring out of the window. A stream of air was blowing his fine, black hair backwards. His dark eyes seemed to be focused a long way away. Chris sat back, so that he wouldn't even be in Nicky's peripheral vision. He hoped he wouldn't dislike what he was about to hear.

'I reckon the problem was that we were too close. Everyone was thinking about us as if we were twins or something. Remember?'

Chris could recall it very well. When Ray Foulds, the United scout, had first approached them, he had made it very clear that he was most impressed by the way they worked together. He had seen them play an important Cup game for the school, and it had been their natural partnership that had set up a close-fought victory.

Surely that meant it was their close friendship that had got them in in the first place! Was Nicky really suggesting that it was a problem instead?

'So, on the day, we both had to do well, or neither of us was going to make it, right? And, let's face it, it wasn't one of your better days.'

Chris's mouth opened automatically, ready to let him remind Nicky just who had been acting like a spoiled brat, and just who had allowed himself to get distracted. This was typical Nicky! He never took responsibility for his own actions, he always tried to shift the blame, he always —

Chris realised Nicky had turned round and was looking back at him with a slight smile creasing his face.

76

'I know, some of it was my fault. We'd had that argument, and I was still carrying a grudge. I didn't have a great day either.'

Chris's mouth shut with an audible clunk.

Nicky faced the front of the bus again, looking relaxed and calm as he recalled the incidents that had almost driven them to become enemies. Chris decided that whatever this conversation was leading towards, it wasn't going to rehash the old arguments.

'I reckon it's been good for us, this last year, playing half the time in different teams,' Nicky explained. 'I mean, we had a brilliant season at school, but we weren't in each other's pockets, you know?'

Chris didn't reply. Everything Nicky had said so far (well, at least in the last few moments) made sense. He wanted to see where this was leading.

'I've really enjoyed playing with Gainsbury. They play a really straightforward game there, you know? Short passes, lots of running off the ball. It means I've always got options. I've learned I don't always have to split the defence with a killer thirty-metre pass, or beat a defender three times waiting for the rest of the attack to get up. At Spirebrook, it always feels like the only outlet I have when I've got the ball is you.'

Chris thought he could see what Nicky was driving at. In some ways, he felt the same too. The Colts were a completely different outfit to Spirebrook, and it was Rory Blackstone who took the central striker's role, not Chris.

When Iain Walsh had first told Chris that he wanted his new player to work wider, almost as an orthodox winger, but with the licence to come inside if there was space, Chris had wondered if he had made a mistake. That feeling lasted for as long as it took to score the first goal. Whole new possibilities opened up playing alongside Rory, who was the most unselfish partner Chris had ever known. He'd lost count of the number of knock-downs he'd run on to; or the number of times he had found space while the central defenders were trying to keep control of Rory.

'I think I know what you mean,' he told Nicky.

Nicky was smiling. He sat back in the seat, clutching his school bag in his lap.

'I think we'll get through this time. We're better players together, and we're just as good apart. I think they'll take us both. And then – watch out! Can you imagine what it would be like, both of us playing for United at last?'

Chris half-closed his eyes. For the last who-knows-how-many years, he had been able to have this particular daydream at will. But today, when he looked into that special place inside where he kept his ambitions and hopes, there was nothing. Chris couldn't see beyond the trial. And when he thought of the trial, all he could think was, Am I good enough?

Worst of all, when he asked himself that question, the answer he received was 'no'.

'Yes,' said Nicky, and Chris came back to the real world with a bump. He looked across at Nicky who was looking right back, seeming very puzzled.

'Yes what?'

'Yes, you are good enough,' said Nicky. 'Of course you are! Didn't you listen to what I was saying before?'

Chris answered quickly before Nicky started to go through it all again.

'You nervous about Saturday?' Nicky asked. Chris knew Nicky was still completely nerveless about the trial.

'Maybe,' said Chris.

Nicky was surprised, but he put Chris's hesitancy down to the injured arm. 'That's not going to hold you up, is it?' he asked. Chris told him that a lot of the soreness had passed already. He was sure he'd be fine.

'We'll get a bit of last-minute practice in on Friday,' Nicky assured him, satisfied that this was all Chris needed. After that they let the conversation drop until the bus set them down in the city centre and they could walk briskly over the bridge to the ground.

They hit the first obstacle right away. The museum was closed.

'It was open on a Monday before,' wailed Nicky.

'That was on a school trip,' Chris reminded him. 'Maybe they don't allow people to just walk in off the street otherwise.'

This was small consolation to Nicky. Chris could feel that it was about to be his fault that they hadn't checked.

'Maybe we could leave a message or something,' said Chris, heading towards a smaller door at the end of the block. Behind this, there was a small office that handled season ticket sales and other bookings. Chris spoke to the woman behind the glass screen, but he could see he wasn't making much sense as far as she was concerned.

Just when the prospect of trying to persuade Nicky to explore the streets around the stadium was beginning to loom in front of Chris like a stop sign in front of a car with no brakes, a very welcome face appeared in the doorway behind the woman.

'I thought I recognised your voice.'

'Hi, Sean,' Chris replied.

Priest stepped into the woman's office, which pretty much filled the available space. She shot him a disgruntled glance.

'You're a bit early for the trials,' said Priest, grinning.

'And in the wrong place – yeah, I know . . .'

'What are you after?'

Chris took a moment to think about just how to phrase the next bit. There was a nagging doubt in the back of his mind that said United wouldn't sign up anyone who was barking mad. Chris had shared a lot with Sean Priest in the past, and he trusted the youth team manager completely, but perhaps this wasn't the time to mention that they'd come to find out if a ghost had ever played for Oldcester United.

'We're trying to find out about someone who played for the club a long time ago. It's a sort of project.'

'For school? Don't you guys break up tomorrow?'

'It's a kind of holiday project,' explained Chris, which didn't seem too much of a lie. Behind him, Nicky muttered something about Chris needing a holiday.

'So, what do you need to find out?'

'How easy would it be to track down the name of someone who might have played for the club a long time ago?'

'How long? Doris has been here a long time? Would she know him?'

The woman looked at Chris over the rim of her glasses, almost daring him to think of some wise remark.

'No . . .' Chris said carefully, but he couldn't help adding, 'He'd be even – much! – much older than her.'

Too late. Doris had caught the remark and was about to give Chris a piece of her mind. Priest patted her on the shoulder and said something calming in a low voice that Chris didn't quite catch. Whatever it was, it did the trick. Doris's face lost its brittle sharpness and softened into a smile. Perhaps, thought Chris, it would be worth finding out what Priest had said so that he could use it when he next had a run-in with Spirebrook's head, Mrs Cole.

'The club has a lot of its records on computer,' Priest told him. 'But they only go back to the 1960s. How far back do you need to go?'

'Before the war,' Nicky cut in, flashing his most ingratiating smile at Doris. That left only Chris she didn't like.

'Well, there are records of the 1920s and 1930s,' said Priest, 'and if you speak to Doris nicely, maybe she'll look them up for you.'

'The First World War,' Chris said abruptly. Priest was confused. Doris looked at Chris as if he was something she'd found on the bottom of her shoe.

'The First . . ?' Priest asked, unable to even say it, let alone understand it. 'You'll be lucky. I'm not sure there's anything in the place that old.'

Chris mentioned the photograph in the museum. He was sure there were other mementos in the same case.

'Well, you're welcome to take a look,' said Sean, 'but I'm willing to bet that that's all you'll find up there. Go round to the main door and I'll let you in.'

Doris gave him a look which bordered between relief that everyone would be getting out of her way and impatience with Sean's easy-going ways. Chris imagined that she wouldn't have let a first team player into the ground unless he had an appointment.

They met up with Sean at the main doors. He locked up behind them.

'I can only spare about fifteen minutes in any case,' he said briskly. 'I'm meeting someone later.'

Nicky whispered to Chris, wondering if it was a girlfriend.

Chris managed not to laugh and they followed Priest to the

stairs, starting the familiar climb up to the floor which led to the directors' gallery, the dining room and the museum.

'Wouldn't it have made more sense if all this had been on the ground floor?' grumbled Nicky.

'Not my department to make decisions like that,' replied Priest. 'We can take a rest if you need one. Perhaps you're not as fit as I thought.'

Chris was left behind as the two of them raced up the last couple of flights.

Obstacle number two. The museum itself was locked.

Priest managed to find Mr Lively's secretary. She explained that only he, the commercial director and the stadium manager had keys to open the museum. The latter two had already left for the day, and Mr Lively was in a meeting.

'Looks like you're sunk, lads,' explained Priest, with an urgent look at his watch.

At that moment, they all heard a nearby door open, and voices growing in volume. Mr Lively stepped out through the door of his secretary's office, talking back over his shoulder to someone. This second person entered the hall a moment later.

'Blimey,' said Nicky.

Chris had recognised him as well. Apart from his appearance on the pitch on Saturday, the man's face was recognisable from any number of newspaper articles and TV shows.

'Ah! Sean . . . that's a bit of luck,' boomed Mr Lively, who had a rich, full voice that could deafen rock 'n' roll bands three miles away. 'I was hoping to catch you before you left.'

Priest looked genuinely surprised, but recovered quickly, stepping forward to shake Mr Lively's guest by the hand.

'I didn't know you were coming here today, Mr Branson,' he said.

The Virgin boss was smiling warmly as he greeted Priest. The two of them had obviously got to know each other well.

'It's not an official visit or anything,' Branson said. 'I was just down the road talking to some snack manufacturers.'

'Virgin crisps?' Nicky wondered out loud.

Branson noticed the two boys for the first time. 'Are these two of your youth team players, Sean?' he asked.

'Not yet,' replied Priest. 'They live in hope, though.'

'So they could be two of the first students at the new school, then,' Branson remarked. He addressed his next question to Chris. 'How do you feel about that?'

Chris couldn't manage to put anything into words, but Nicky stepped in. 'It'll be great,' he said. 'We finish at our old school tomorrow. After the trial next weekend, we'll be all ready to start at the new school in September –'

'If you get through!' scolded Priest, which Nicky ignored. Richard Branson raised a more important objection.

'The new school won't actually open in September . . .' He hesitated, obviously waiting for someone to supply him with the name of the person he was speaking to.

'Nicky,' Priest added, after a moment's delay.

'Fiorentino,' Mr Lively chipped in, showing what a good memory he had for names, even when they were the wrong ones.

'We have to get the building completed and equipped; we have to hire the staff and work out timetables. We don't expect to open before Easter next year. Maybe later.'

Nicky was reeling from the damage to his dreams of walking out of Spirebrook the next day, never to return.

'Then, what . . ?' he stumbled.

'The trials are the same as normal, Nicky,' explained Priest. 'A chance to find the best players for the youth team. They're a bit special this year, I admit, because the boys on our books will have automatic entry into the new school. Until it's built, though, it's school as usual for all of you.'

Nicky's dark eyes were even darker than usual after he had taken this in. Chris could imagine the storm that was brewing.

'So, what brings these two here again, Sean?' asked Mr Lively, filling the sudden silence.

'Oh, these two are looking for some information about players at the club from before World War One,' Priest explained. Branson looked quite stunned at the news, but Mr Lively took it in his stride.

'Interesting! Well, of course the club's history goes back to the last days of the nineteenth century. When it was first founded, all the players were workers for two rival railway companies. That was how the strip was chosen — the two colours from the liveries of the different trains, and stripes to represent railway tracks. They played on a patch of land at a place called Star Junction, where the railway lines of the two companies crossed and branched out after they left Oldcester Central railway station.'

Mr Lively's voice had taken on an excited tone, like a TV pundit preaching on his favourite subject. If allowed to go much further, he would be unstoppable.

'We were interested in who might have played for the club before the war started,' Chris interrupted. 'We're looking for a specific person we think may have done.'

'What's this — a famous ancestor?' said Mr Lively in a jolly voice.

'Something like that.'

Mr Lively's expression took on a sad quality. 'I don't think we can help. All the club's records before 1920 were lost in a fire. What you see in the club museum is pretty well every-thing we have from the early years . . .'

Chris heard Nicky sigh with frustration. These kind of obstructions were not what Nicky expected when they went off on one of their adventures.

'But you've come to the wrong place really. You should talk to Frank Swain. He's kind of the club's unpaid, unofficial historian.' Mr Lively laughed at the thought. 'He collects old programmes, newspapers, anything. He says he's writing the club's history, but I happen to know he's been working on it for thirty-five years and still isn't finished. He'll tell you what you need to know. If you give me a moment, I'll have Lucy find you the address. It's not far . . .'

Chris didn't fancy the prospect of dragging Nicky off to the home of some anorak whose living room floor would be piled with yellowing bits of newspaper and boxes of programmes. He wondered if there was something more immediate he could look at.

'Is there a list of players from back then — like the board in the museum, the one that has all the modern players?'

Mr Lively slapped his forehead with his palm. 'Of course! What am I thinking of? All the older boards are on the wall of my office. Would you like to see them?'

Chris couldn't think of anything he'd like better. Mr Lively almost turned round on the spot to lead the way.

There was a soft cough.

'Richard – so sorry! I got caught up there for a minute.'

'Don't worry about it, Dennis. I think we've done all we can today anyhow. Come down to London next week, and we'll work out the details for that other matter we were discussing.'

It took Mr Lively a moment to remember what that was. 'Right, yes!' he boomed. 'Monday OK with you?'

Branson rubbed his bearded chin and considered the date. 'I think so. Just to be on the safe side, give my office a call. I may be in America.'

That put something else into Dennis Lively's overactive mind.

'Chris here is off to America in a few weeks. Exchange programme. The club fixed it up, but it's actually one of the district teams making the exchange – a team Sean keeps an eye on.'

'I hope you're flying Virgin,' said Branson, smiling. Chris knew the Colts were actually flying out on United, but he decided not to share this with the Virgin boss. The last thing he wanted was the sponsorship deal falling through because the Colts were flying with an American airline. After a while he realised he was being over-cautious, but by then Branson and Mr Lively had said their farewells and Sean was offering to see their guest to the gate.

As soon as the other two men had left, Mr Lively marched Chris and Nicky into his office, pausing briefly to ask his secretary to find an address for Frank Swain. As he opened the door, Chris expected to see something with wooden panels and old furniture, which seemed to be the standard decoration style for any football chairman's office on TV. In fact, Dennis Lively's office was a bright, clean space, with a loud carpet in the club's colours, metal and glass desk, a high-spec computer with a huge monitor, and sharp white lighting from wall fittings. It almost hurt their eyes.

'I've not long had it redecorated,' the United chairman explained. 'It takes a bit of getting used to.'

Nicky remarked that the United manager had been wearing

dark glasses for the last few games of the season. Now they knew why.

Mr Lively was heading for the corner (fortunately, he missed Nicky's sarcastic remark). There was a stack of wooden panels there, leaning against the walls. Chris guessed what they were at once.

'They don't really go with the decorations in here any more,' Mr Lively explained. 'I'm not sure where to put them.' He was leafing through the old boards, looking for the first one in the sequence. 'Perhaps the dining room. Ah – here we are. Come and get hold of this, will you, boys?'

Chris and Nicky stepped up to help, taking hold of the darkest of the four or five boards and pulling it free while Mr Lively held up the others. It was surprisingly heavy. They propped it against a cabinet, facing into the room.

Mr Lively joined them in front of the shiny steel columns that supported his desk. 'I'd forgotten how faded it all was.'

It certainly was. The wood was stained with smoke and the black lettering had faded until it was almost the same, sombre colour. The most recent names were OK, but the further back they read, the harder it became.

'What name are we looking for?' asked Mr Lively.

'William,' replied Nicky, bluntly.

'We had a Brian Williams between the wars,' Mr Lively recalled. 'Right wing. Very quick. Went to play in Spain.'

'William's his first name,' Nicky pointed out.

Mr Lively raised his thick eyebrows. 'Oh. There aren't any first names. Just initials.'

Chris had been expecting that, of course, so he wasn't disappointed about not seeing William's name spelt out. However, the murky lettering was so hard to decipher that even spotting the initial wasn't going to be easy.

'W. Gates,' read Mr Lively. 'Look there, under 1912/13. And again the following season.' He scratched his beard roughly. 'I think I know a bit about him. Came back after the war, I think. Scottish international.'

Nicky jotted the name down anyway. 'Shame we don't have any pictures,' he said in a quiet voice.

'Oh. You know what this fellow looks like, then?' Mr Lively asked him.

'Chris does,' said Nicky, with a bitter sting in his voice.

'Got a photo, have you?' Mr Lively asked. Nicky guffawed loudly.

While the others were distracted Chris found another name. 'W. Jones,' he read out. '1908/09. Just the one season.'

'You only have to have played once to get on here,' Mr Lively commented, making it sound like a great proud principle.

'But it has to be the first team, right?' asked Nicky.

'Of course.'

Chris was edging closer. He'd just noticed something strange.

'The handwriting on the last two names here is different,' he said. 'Look, at the bottom of –' He traced his finger back up to the top of the column '– the 1914/15 season.' It was a very short list of names that year too.

'Of course!' Mr Lively boomed, his voice raising in volume to almost painful levels. 'The 1914/15 season never really got going. We went to war with Germany in August, and the season was suspended pretty well as soon as it started. That's why there are so few names . . . I'm not sure if this lot played more than one or two games.'

He sat back against the desk and pondered something for a moment. His eyes flashed when the memory was triggered.

'I've just remembered something about it now. Can't remember who told me. The old boy who did the lettering back then was an army reservist. He was called up as soon as the war started. That's why these last two names are in a different hand.'

'It's really hard to make them out,' sighed Chris, peering even closer.

'A lot of those lads on there signed up for the army almost as soon as the fighting began. I suppose those two were brought in to make up a team again.'

'I think the second name is Schwarz,' Chris said. 'Initial looks like a "J".'

'No good to us then,' muttered Nicky.

'The other one . . .' Chris squinted, trying to make it out. 'That might be a "W". It looks like it.' He tried to make out the surname. 'Morton? Murton?'

Nicky moved into the way. 'Murdoch,' he decided after the barest glance. Chris didn't feel like asking if he was sure. Nicky went back and wrote it down.

They completed the list and helped Mr Lively stack the board back with the others.

'Did you get what you wanted?' he asked.

Nicky shrugged. They walked to the door.

Chris took one last look back at the wooden panels, and the shadowy image of that name burned into his mind. W. Murdoch. William Murdoch.

'Yes, we did. Thank you, Mr Lively.' He beamed brightly as they left. 'Thank you very much.'

'Are we going to see this Frank Smith now?' asked Nicky as they left the stadium precinct. Chris was looking at the address and the directions Mr Lively's secretary had supplied.

'Swain,' Chris corrected him. 'I don't think so, not tonight. It might take some time for him to find what we're looking for. I'll ring him when we get home and we'll arrange to see him later in the week.'

Nicky agreed, although Chris could see he wasn't thrilled at the prospect of having to waste even a single day of the summer vacation chasing after Chris's ghost.

'So, are we heading back, then?' he asked, his mind turning to visions of dinner.

'I just want to check out the street name William mentioned,' said Chris. 'Warwick Street.'

'Look it up in an A to Z,' said Nicky, offhandedly.

'I did,' said Chris. 'I couldn't find it. William said it was somewhere near the stadium. Well, there's the old estate on the other side of Easter Road, but all the roads there are named after trees and royal castles. Further down, there are some more residential streets, but I couldn't find a Warwick Street.'

'Did you look in the index?' asked Nicky, showing an unusual sense of logic. Chris hated to admit that he hadn't.

'I don't want *any* Warwick Street; it has to be right near the ground.'

'Why?'

'He said something about the shadow of the stadium falling on his house.'

Standing on Easter Road, the boys looked around them at the last of the day's bright sunshine, which was throwing deep shadows across the faces of the shops and flats. Once again showing an amazing burst of intellect, it was Nicky who worked out that for the shadow of the stadium to fall on William's house, Warwick Street would have to be on the north side of the stadium, the opposite side to where they were looking.

It wasn't an area they had ever explored. They didn't even know what was out there. Chris knew they could walk up the riverside path, behind the stand that stood there, but he had no idea where the path led.

'Let's check it out,' said Nicky.

They turned back towards the bridge, then trotted down a long flight of stairs to the river's embankment. The path was wide and well fenced — a necessity since it was where the away supporters waited to pass through the turnstiles into the River End. At the northern end, the gap narrowed as the river curved slightly, coming closer to the corner of the stadium, but a footpath continued along the river.

Once they were past the stadium, they were faced with a wire-topped wall, just high enough to block their view. It looked new, and every now and again there were yellow signs announcing that the wall was coated with anti-climbing paint. Other signs warned them that the premises were guarded by Sentinel Security, whoever they were.

'So what is it, do you think?' whispered Nicky, who clearly had it down as a secret government spy centre.

Chris had no idea, but he thought he could see how they could find out. Two plastic milk crates were floating in the river near the bank.

'Grab them, Nicky. Let's make something we can climb on.'

A few other bits of rubbish were collected, which allowed them to make a precarious platform tall enough to allow them to see over the top of the wall.

'Up you go, then,' said Nicky.

'Why me?'

'This is your project,' Nicky insisted quickly, pulling a face. 'Besides, you're taller than I am.'

Chris considered this for a moment. 'Be fair, Nicky. I can't climb with my arm in a sling. What if I slipped? I'd have nothing to catch myself with.'

Nicky looked at Chris's arm, frowning deeply. It looked like a winning argument. And they had made the structure tall enough so Nicky would have a perfectly good view over the wall.

He tested the wall with the tip of his finger, trying to discover what anti-climbing paint did. There was no alarm, explosion or electric shock, so he put one foot on the junk pile to test it, then slowly pushed himself up. He stooped at first, trying to make sure that his head wouldn't be visible over the wall, then gradually straightened so that he could peek inside. Chris held a hand against his back to help his team mate steady himself.

'It's just offices,' he announced. Nicky's idea of a spy centre would have included a few radar dishes at the very least. 'A big car park and —'

'Oi!'

The voice was fierce and ugly. It said 'security guard' all over it. Even though Chris couldn't see anything, he jolted back with panic. Nicky felt his grip go, and grabbed at the top of the wall to prevent himself from falling.

'Oh, man!!!' he wailed.

The ugly voice was calling again, ordering him to stop. Chris watched as Nicky glowered across the wall.

'Oh, shut up, you poor man's excuse for a policeman! Just because you've got a uniform, doesn't make you God, you know!'

Chris heard the guard's voice growing even more aggressive. It was much closer now.

'What are you going to do?' mocked Nicky. 'We're out here and you're in there. It's not as if we were trying to break in or anything. We were just having a look!'

'Come back here!' roared the man.

Nicky poked out his tongue and dropped down from the rubbish stack. He held out his hands towards Chris. 'Look!' he wailed.

Below the wrists, his hands were coated with a browny-black oil, almost as thick as tar. Some of it had dripped down on to the cuffs of his shirt, and there were smears on the front of his jacket.

'Yuck!' exclaimed Chris. 'Don't touch anything!'

He found some old newspaper among the other litter and they managed to get some of the worst oil off Nicky's hands. The rest stuck like glue.

'There are some loos on Easter Road,' Chris remembered. 'We'll wash it off in there.'

They started to walk away, Nicky holding his hands out like he was carrying an invisible box. Chris stifled a small chuckle, but not well enough.

'What?' Nicky demanded.

Chris didn't reply. He could hardly tell his mate that after all the times Chris's jacket had been soiled, ripped or soaked during fights or other scrapes Nicky had caused or been at the centre of, it seemed quite appropriate that Nicky had finally had a share of the problem. It was unlikely that Nicky would see the funny side of it.

'That's stupid that is!' Nicky yelled as they passed one of the yellow warning signs. 'It's not anti-climbing paint. It doesn't stop you climbing at all. You just get filthy if you do.' He glared at Chris, daring him to offer a different opinion. 'Stupid! They should say what they mean!' he concluded.

'Hey, you two! Stop right there!'

An invisible security guard was very low on Nicky's list of priorities right then, but he snapped back 'Get lost, Hitler!' immediately. It took them another half-second to realise the voice had come from directly behind them.

A gate in the wall. Sneaky, but effective. The guard was out on the embankment, just twenty metres away. If he hadn't been the type who thinks that yelling always gets results, he could have sneaked up on them without their knowing a thing about it.

'Run!' yelled Chris, pointlessly, since Nicky was off ahead of him. The brief glimpse they had had of the guard confirmed that he was at least 50, about six foot two, grey haired and overweight. Ordinarily, he would have posed no threat at all in a flat sprint, but both boys were handicapped by their arms.

Nicky was still carrying his imaginary parcel, while Chris had his right arm close to his chest. Their awkward gaits were slowing them down. Even so, they were fit enough to open a steadily wider gap by the time they reached the stairs.

They pounded up three at a time, reaching the street with a gap that felt nearer 30 metres than twenty. Chris looked right and left, assessing their chances either way. Across the bridge to the right, the pavement was fairly quiet, and they would be able to sprint flat out. However, they'd also be in clear sight. He wondered if anyone would see two boys being chased by a security guard and decide to lend a hand.

The other way led directly past the shops and houses fronting Easter Road, and the gateway into the precinct of Star Park. There were more people there, more places to hide. Chris elected to go left.

Inevitably, Nicky went the other way.

There was a moment when they both turned, hesitated and called at each other to follow. Then they both saw the guard's peaked cap and decided to go with their first instincts.

Chris dropped his pace, tried not to look so worried, and slipped into the crowds. He didn't look back until he was 50 metres along the road, coming up to the main entrance to the ground. When he stole a glance over his shoulder, he couldn't see any signs of pursuit, so he ducked into a chemist to hide while he recovered his breath.

He bought some M&Ms while he was waiting.

No-one followed him in. Chris decided the guard must have gone after Nicky. That made sense – Nicky was the one he had seen over the wall. Perhaps he could just step out, walk over to the bus stop and put some real distance between himself and the guard.

He blew a long sigh of relief.

The guard clapped his hands on Chris the second he stepped out on to the street. Chris could barely believe it. The guy came out of nowhere, like a ghost (which was a most inappropriate thing to think of, in the circumstances).

'Got you,' he snarled.

91

Startled, Chris looked up into the guy's face. It wasn't a pleasant sight. He had yellowing fangs that were so narrow and spaced out they looked more like spiked railings than teeth. His eyes were wet, red and bulging. His face was red too, and sweating with the effort of chasing after Chris and Nicky. He smelled of cigarettes and stale sweat.

His fist was gripping Chris's jacket so tight there was no way to escape. Chris was almost lifted off his feet.

'Thought you were clever, didn't you?' the man snarled. 'Sneaking into the shop like that, but I saw you!'

'Let me go!' Chris yelled back, fighting against the man's grip. 'I haven't done anything!'

'No you haven't! That's because I caught you in time! I hate little brats like you, who think they can just do what they want and then escape without facing the consequences. I bet you thought I'd given up, eh? Well, I never give up. Sooner or later, I always catch the ones I want.'

Chris wriggled, but he was stuck tight. It didn't seem very likely that reasoning with the guard would have much effect either. Chris wondered what he could do . . .

'Excuse me,' came a voice. 'Just what is going on here?'

A smartly dressed young woman had entered the discussion. She was about 30, with short, dark hair. There was a strong, determined look about her face that Chris decided was a lot more attractive than the guard's ugly expression. Not a tricky decision at all.

'Stay out of this!' the guard snapped at her, which immediately ensured that she stayed very firmly in it.

'Why have you grabbed this boy?'

'What's it got to do with you, you nosy cow?'

The guard clearly liked to get people on his side. Chris could afford to keep quiet for the moment, allowing Pin Teeth to dig a deeper hole for himself while Chris gathered his thoughts.

'I'm a solicitor. I know what the law is in these cases. What reason do you have for arresting this boy?'

Arrest didn't sound good to Chris. Could he be arrested by this uniformed thug? Bearing in mind that he and Nicky had been on the edge of doing stuff they shouldn't, was having a lawyer involved such a good thing?

'He was trying to get over the fence into the Science and Technology Park. Him and a mate. I saw 'em, and chased them up here. His mate's legged it over the bridge, but I followed this one and saw him coming out of the chemist.'

The case for the prosecution having been made, the woman turned her attention to Chris. There was a growing group of people around them rubber-necking who could have made a jury.

'Is this true?' the woman asked.

'No!' insisted Chris. 'I've been visiting the football ground — you can ask someone there!'

As soon as he'd said it, Chris wished he hadn't. He knew Sean Priest had gone home. The last thing he wanted was to bother Dennis Lively. If Chris still had any belief that he might sign forms for United, he couldn't afford to give the chairman the idea that he might be some kind of burglar or vandal.

'I've never been in the Science and Technology Park,' he insisted, which was true. 'And look!' he said, inspiration coming into his mind. He lifted his right arm slightly, making sure everyone on the jury could see the sling. A rustle of comment went round the crowd.

'I can't climb with that,' he added.

'He could just be faking!' the guard insisted, keeping Chris in his grip.

'No, look, I've got these pain-killers and everything.' Chris dived into his jacket pocket and fetched them out. It did no harm to his case that everyone could see the chemist's bag in the same pocket (even if all it contained was a packet of M&Ms).

The woman looked at the small plastic tub with Doctor Loenikov's label and handwritten instructions and gave it back to Chris.

'Are you sure you've got the right boy?' she asked.

Pin Teeth was still unhappy to have her involved and he allowed his resentment to show.

'Of course! I chased him up here, didn't I?'

'Did the boy you were chasing have a sling on his arm?' she replied, her voice cultured. She was completely in control.

There wasn't an easy answer to that, Chris realised. If Pin Teeth had seen Chris had a sling on his arm, he should have

93

realised he couldn't have climbed anyway. If he answered 'no', then he'd be saying Chris wasn't the right boy. Chris had to admire the woman's technique. This was better than watching *Kavanagh QC*.

'There's special paint on the walls!' the guard insisted. 'He'll have it on him!'

Chris winced with pain as the man pulled at his hands, looking for the tell-tale paint. Luckily, he'd kept far enough back from Nicky so that there wasn't any. Pin Teeth didn't give up, but when he started to pull at Chris's sling, making Chris yelp with pain, the woman decided she had had enough.

'Stop that right now! You've clearly made a mistake!'

Not as much as the one he was about to make.

'I've told you, woman – keep out of this!'

'And I've told you, let the boy go!' Her eyes flickered across the front of his uniform, looking for an ID badge. 'What's your name? I'm going to report you to your employers.'

Pin Teeth hissed at her defiantly, but Chris actually felt the guard's grip loosen on his jacket.

'Mind your own business!'

'Have it your way. Your uniform says Sentinel Security. I'll just call them. They can't have that many morons working for them that look like you.'

She had a mobile phone in her hand, ready to dial. The crowd around them seemed to have decided that she was right, too. Pin Teeth looked around them, his jaw clamped firmly shut. After a moment, he let Chris go.

'Your lucky day,' he snarled. Chris decided that maybe it was. Certainly the injury to his arm was proving to be a lucky break after all. Or a lucky strain, at least.

'No, it's yours,' the woman snapped. 'You're lucky I don't press charges against you for assault on this boy. I suggest you keep your mouth shut, turn around and go.'

Pin Teeth clearly had a problem taking orders from a woman, but there was no way to win this argument. He slipped away gradually.

Chris watched him go.

'I'm really grateful,' he told the woman.

'Try scrumping for apples next time,' she said, winking. '

work at the park, and I know what those guards are like. Just keep away from the place, OK?'

Chris smiled back at her. She asked where he was headed and walked with him over to the bus stop. 'Straight home now, promise?' she demanded. Chris thanked her.

That's enough, he told himself as the bus drew up and he stepped on board. This William business has got to stop. I don't need any of this aggravation.

It was a decision and a promise he meant to keep. It lasted just as long as it took for the bus to get to the other side of Oldcester's city centre, near to the railway station. Not long after that, however, Chris wondered if he shouldn't have taken the solicitor's advice and gone scrumping after all.

Thirteen

The bus crawled along the north side of Fair Market, along St James Street. The traffic was solid. Chris stared out of the window wondering if Nicky had got home yet. He'd have to call him as soon as he got back.

It was starting to get a little darker outside. Chris hoped that he wasn't going to be late for dinner again.

At the roundabout at the end of St James Street, the bus turned left on to White Hill Road, towards the railway station, from where it would begin the run out towards Spirebrook. Chris continued to look out of the window, watching the lights in shops and offices as they passed.

At the north end of the station, he noticed that some work had started on a major rebuilding project, designed to use some redundant British Railway land as the centre of a new conference centre and exhibition hall. A small number of houses were also being knocked down — Victorian terraces along short streets between the main road and the railway. He noticed a couple of the names — Kenilworth Street, Coventry Street. Chris saw all the houses were already empty, boarded up and awaiting demolition.

Even as he noticed that fact, a small warning bell went off in the back of his mind. There was something he'd missed, something that should have made sense, if only he'd been paying attention.

He looked out of the window again. The bus was moving towards a second roundabout, from where it would turn right on to the road which led out towards the university and then to Spirebrook. The last of the abandoned, darkened streets was passing by. Aston Street.

That was curious. Aston and Coventry, two Premiership

sides in the West Midlands. And Kenilworth Road was the name of Luton Town's ground. What a strange coincidence.

Chris realised why it wasn't a coincidence and the reason for the alarm bell in the same second. The streets weren't named after some football connection; these were towns in the West Midlands. Aston, Kenilworth, Coventry . . . and Warwick.

He flew down the stairs, ringing the bell furiously for the bus to stop. The driver shot him an angry glance, but Chris ignored him. He'd made the connection. There was no Warwick Street in the shadow of Star Park because that wasn't the home ground William had been talking about. He'd meant the old home of Oldcester United, the team created by the railway workers.

That first stadium had been on the railway's land, near the main station. The houses being demolished for the new conference centre had stood in its shadow. Even though he hadn't seen it, Chris knew that one of those old, short streets, lined on either side with small back-to-back houses, was Warwick Street.

The bus came to a halt. Chris jumped from the platform, crossed the road and ran past the roundabout, back the way he had just come. At the end of Aston Street, he took a long look to see what he was dealing with. There was a wire fence across the street, set back about 10 metres from the main road. Signs warned parents not to allow their children to wander on to the site. Aston Street's houses were demolished already, the site levelled flat in preparation for the new building.

He ran steadily back along White Hill Road. The shops were all closed, except for a corner off-licence and a laundromat. Only the constant hum of the passing cars broke the stillness of this silent part of the city, waiting for its new life to begin.

Kenilworth and Leamington Streets had been levelled as completely as Aston Street. There was a JCB parked just beyond the fence. Chris saw a commuter train rattle across in the distance beyond the end of the road. He ran on.

There wasn't a soul in sight, save the drivers of the cars, slowly inching their way towards the junctions at either end of this short, connecting road. Chris doubted that any of them even noticed their surroundings as they came through. This would just be a grim part of the journey, through an abandoned area, finally being redeveloped into something worthwhile. Chris could only think of it as a ghost town.

Coventry Street hadn't yet been completely razed to the ground. The last dozen houses on either side were still standing, though they were boarded up and empty. Chris also noticed that the fence wasn't very well put up across this road; two of the panels were slightly skewed, leaving a small space between them that someone small could get through.

Chris wasn't interested in that, though. There was one more side street off this road. If he was right . . .

He ran the last block a little faster, a buzz of anticipation in his guts. It was like knowing the answer to a question in an exam the second you turned the paper over. He knew he was right.

But when he reached the last turning, there was no street sign. It had been removed. Once again, there were a dozen or more abandoned houses on each side of the street, just behind the fence. A small fire was burning on a mound of earth and rubble a little way beyond them.

'Great!' muttered Chris. So near and yet so far. He stood in front of the fence, his one good hand on his hip, staring at the firelight through the metal grid. He couldn't complete the puzzle, just because of some missing street signs. It occurred to him that all he had to do was find an old street map. If it showed this was Warwick Street it would confirm his theory just as completely but he still felt cheated.

'You're a hard man to find, William,' he muttered, and it was as he drew breath at the end of that sentence that he saw him.

At first, it could have been anyone. It was just a silhouette in front of the fire, walking slowly through the strewn bricks and broken paving stones. Tall, male, almost cat-like in the way he crossed the ground. It might have been someone scavenging among the rubble, or some teenager up to mischief. But Chris knew different.

'William!' he called. 'William!'

The dark outline seemed to pause for a moment, then moved hurriedly away to one side, out of sight beyond the last of the houses. Chris banged his hand against the metal fence in frustration.

The gap. The gap in the fence.

He turned and ran back to Coventry Street as if his life depended on it.

When he reached the buckled fence, he realised at once that he was looking at a very small gap. He didn't need to test it – he could tell at once that it would be a tight squeeze. He looked up, considering climbing over, but the fence was high and didn't look that safe. He tried moving the panels further apart, but even though he gave it all he had, the gap opened less than a millimetre.

That left one option.

Chris removed his sling and jacket, and thrust them into his school bag. At least, with it being the end of term, that was mostly empty. He thrust the bag through the gap, then sat down on the floor to figure out the best way through the hole. Head first seemed to make sense.

Turning so that he was on the shoulder of his good arm, Chris wriggled into the gap, pulling himself through by taking hold of the panel and levering himself along. It wasn't easy. He was almost too wide across the shoulders to get through the hole and it took a lot of heaving and squirming to get his body through. Then his trousers snagged on a piece of sharp metal, which Chris had to extricate himself from.

Finally, he was inside. Grabbing his bag, he ran along the rubble-strewn street, past the end of the remaining houses, then right, towards the matching terraces of what Chris hoped was Warwick Street. Ahead, the fire was dying down. No-one was in sight – no workers, no scavengers and no ghosts.

Was that good news or bad? Chris asked himself.

There was a wall beside Chris to the right, the top of which ran at head height. He looked over it as he scampered over the uneven ground, wondering if William had entered one of the abandoned houses. He couldn't see anything in the small yards at the back of each house. A narrow alley ran between the yards of Coventry and Warwick Streets, clogged with rubbish and waste from the demolition of the rest of the two streets.

Chris moved on. At last he reached Warwick Street, able to look back towards the main road through the fence he had been the other side of just fifteen minutes before.

'So, now what?' he asked out loud.

No-one answered, and Chris realised that he really didn't know what he was doing here. Should he call out again? Whistle?

What was he trying to prove? If he caught up with William again, what was he going to do – ask him if he was a ghost or an escaped lunatic? At the very least William lived a very eccentric lifestyle. Why was Chris interested in him at all? Why was he risking so much to find out?

'Why am I asking myself all these questions?' he muttered, clenching his teeth. 'I'm either looking for him or I'm not. What else am I doing here?'

He started to narrow down his options. When he last saw William (What should he refer to William as? The ghost? The man? The ex-footballer?), he had been walking in front of the fire, from right to left. He'd disappeared behind the houses on the left. So, did that mean he lived in one of these houses (now or in the past)? What was he doing here?

Beyond the northern side of Warwick Street, at the back of the small terraced houses, there was a high wall and a grim, empty factory which had been largely destroyed in a fire. This too was scheduled for demolition as part of the redevelopment. The wall didn't look climbable, and Chris couldn't see that there would be much attraction in going into the factory's burnt-out shell. There was no roof, and some of the walls were leaning at very peculiar angles as if the old place couldn't wait for the wrecking crews to arrive.

So, Chris decided, William had to have been coming from one of the houses on that northern side of Warwick Street. Some of them were still intact; a few even had odd panes of glass in the windows. Perhaps William had been squatting in one?

Assuming, of course, that he was discounting the idea that William had last lived here 80 years ago.

Chris looked around, trying to gauge where the old stadium

might have been, but there weren't any clues. However, it seemed possible that the railway yards had once extended over almost all of this area, which meant that perhaps these houses weren't what was left of the street, they were all there had ever been. Was it possible that Chris was actually standing on the entrance into Oldcester United's first ground?

There would be a way of finding that out, Chris decided. Old maps. Something in the club museum, perhaps.

For now, the houses were the key. He made his way over to the nearest.

The front door had been replaced by a single sheet of solid hardboard, nailed into place. It didn't budge an inch when Chris tried it. The front windows, which had once looked out directly on to the pavement, were also boarded up. Chris stepped back. The next house looked just as tightly barred, although there was an open upstairs window. Short of suddenly being able to fly, though, Chris knew he couldn't get in that way.

The third house had prospects. Instead of a hardboard sheet, the windows were covered with just a sheet of plastic.

Chris walked over. One corner was flapping gently in the breeze. He lifted it, and realised that the staples holding that entire side had pulled through from the rotten window frame. He pulled the sheet back.

He could see nothing, of course. The evening was just starting to darken and there wasn't enough light to illuminate inside. He might be able to get into the house, but he wouldn't be able to find anything. If only he had some matches –

The fire.

It was just about still alight. Chris dropped his bag and ran to the bonfire. On the way he collected some old newspaper which he twisted to make short-lived torches. He stored six or seven of these in his belt. There was a lot of junk smouldering and glowing on the pile, from which a thick brown-grey column of smoke was still rising. Chris found some twigs, broken planks and floorboards, and a few other items which might just hold a fire. Dragging them back to the house he had found, he managed to fan a spark from the bonfire into something that would set light to a newspaper twist, then carried this back to his own, smaller bonfire. He managed to get it to light. Finally, he had a ready source of illumination.

Once again, he pulled back the plastic sheeting on the window. The flickering light revealed nothing more than a bare, empty room.

The sense of disappointment after all his hard work was almost enough to make Chris scream. It took him several moments to calm down. What had he expected? A furnished living room?

He decided to explore, and stepped over the low window-sill into the abandoned house.

Now that he was inside, he could see that there were scraps of wallpaper and other signs that this was once someone's home. The fireplace had a wooden shelf along the top; there was a deep gouge in the plaster where a picture nail had been removed; Chris even found some damp, mouldy curtains piled in the corner.

He tested the floorboards carefully, but they appeared sound enough. He walked slowly across the room, through the open doorway and into a tiny hall. There was a back room, a cramped kitchen and a back door leading out into the yard. He also noticed a cupboard under the stairs.

His first torch was getting a little low, so he pulled another twist of paper from his belt and lit that from the first.

The brighter light revealed that the stairs appeared to be solid enough. Chris decided to chance his arm (an expression he regretted as soon as he thought of it). Reaching out for the banister, he started to climb.

To his continued relief, the house was still solid enough, and he didn't plunge to his doom through the staircase. He wondered how long it had been empty.

At the top of the flight, there was a short landing. The room at the back had been gutted – Chris imagined it must once have been the bathroom. The door to the front bedroom was closed. When Chris tried it, he found it was wedged so tight it wouldn't open. Giving up on that, he took a quick look into the box room at the front. Nothing there.

Which left the back room. That door too seemed locked or jammed, but it gave a little when Chris tried it, so he put his shoulder to it and tried again. At the third attempt the door fell open. Chris knew at once that he had found something.

There was a sleeping bag on the floor, tucked against the wall. Beside it, there was an empty tin of baked beans, a small plate, a metal fork, a can opener, matches, candles, a tobacco tin, and a dirty pair of jeans and a ragged old jumper.

Although this was hardly the most impressive find in the world, Chris was strangely excited. There was nothing that linked this stuff to William – and if it was his, it scuppered the ghost theory – but Chris felt a small buzz in his mind that convinced him he was close to something important.

The most useful prize in the first instance, of course, were the candles. The boarded windows didn't let even a scrap of light in. Chris quickly crossed the room and selected the largest of the candles, lighting it from the newspaper twist he was carrying.

Now that the room was more safely illuminated, Chris crouched down on the bare boards to consider what to do next. The sleeping bags and the other stuff lay in front of him. He knew he couldn't bring himself to search them – it just wouldn't be right invading someone's privacy like that. Whoever it was, he (or she) didn't exactly live a fun-packed life as things were, without Chris rifling through his or her meagre possessions. Having made that decision, Chris turned round to face the door, so that he would see if anyone came back. He was pretty sure, now, that the person he had seen moving across in front of the fire was squatting in this house. It wasn't much, but it was somehow reassuring to know that his mind wasn't playing tricks. If it wasn't William, that would explain why he hadn't answered. Or . . .

Chris froze. The glow of the candle wasn't exactly bright, but his eyes had adjusted to the partial gloom and he could see the room quite clearly now. It didn't have any furniture as such, although a tea chest served as a kind of table beside the sleeping bag. However, it had clearly once been a child's bedroom – there were scraps of Dungeons and Dragons wallpaper on some of the walls. In most places, though, the paper had been scraped clean or was peeled back to reveal the plaster beneath.

What had caught Chris's eye was a cluster of drawings and

writing on the plaster in one corner. He picked up the candle and moved closer, intrigued by what he had seen. Closer, his initial impression was confirmed.

The drawings featured stick men in football kit playing football. In the largest picture, a player in a striped shirt, better drawn than the others, was scoring a goal, having weaved past six defenders. Other drawings showed an angry figure, labelled 'JS', fallen on his backside while the stick man in the stripes ran past, or a goalkeeper crying as the striped shirt guy headed a goal.

The writing beside the pictures was faded, but it was still distinct close up. In large, even capital letters, it said OLDCESTER UNITED 191914. A phone number? Then, underneath, there was a list of eleven names in smaller handwriting. Chris knew at once what he was looking at – a team list.

What made the list even more intriguing was that Chris recognised some of the names. One of them jumped out at him immediately – 'W. Murdoch'. The name he and Nicky had found on the board. The longer he looked at the wall, the more sure he became that the other names he thought he recognised were from the same board. That was when the idea came to him that the number at the top wasn't a telephone number, it was a date. The first of September 1914.

William's game for Oldcester United.

Chris's heart was beating fast. This was the proof he needed. Somehow, he had to find Nicky, get him to come and see this. Or Rory's camera. He had to record this evidence somehow.

He had no doubts that it was genuine. On the walls of Chris's own home there were similar drawings and doodles under the paper – outlines to show how he'd grown over the years; cartoon pictures his father had drawn of Mickey Mouse, Bugs Bunny and a strange egg-headed creature peering over a wall.

He searched his pockets, finding a pen but no paper. He had plenty, of course, out in his bag. He decided to go and get it.

The candle lit his way downstairs. As he reached the hall, it also showed him that the door to the cupboard under the stairs was partly ajar. That was odd. Hadn't it been closed tight before?

He paused, then gingerly reached out for the edge of the door and pulled it open. Nothing leapt out. He opened the door wider and peered inside.

He was surprised to see that it wasn't a cupboard, but a stairway. It was narrow and steep, leading down to a cellar. There were thick cobwebs all over the walls and ceilings. The light from the candle didn't reach far enough to show what might be down there, but Chris decided he wasn't going to look. How many films had he watched where someone walked into a house, knowing that some crazed serial killer or blood-sucking vampire might be inside?

And what happened next? The aforementioned killer/ vampire jumped them and that was that. Did the victims ever think of staying outside and waiting for morning, or calling for back-up? No . . .

Chris wasn't going to fall into that particular trap. He'd managed to get into enough trouble already. Instinctively, he started to look at his watch, but just as quickly he decided he really didn't want to know the time.

He had to hurry. There was an old tin box on a shelf, next to some pipes and a meter that looked ancient enough to have measured coal or straw or whatever they had before electricity. Chris picked it up.

The box had something inside. Chris opened the lid and found a small book inside. It had a black leather cover and yellowed, crumbling pages. The stitching along the spine had rotted, so that the individual pages were loose, held together more by habit than anything physical.

Chris wanted to read it there and then, but a combination of tin, candle and fragile book was too much for someone with only one and a half arms, so he decided to check it out later. He had a more important job to do now; namely getting some paper to record the names on the wall upstairs. Replacing the book in the tin, he went quickly into the front room and out through the window, pressing back the plastic sheet. He dropped the tin into his bag and searched for the A4 pad he knew was inside.

Which was when he realised that he wasn't alone. There was a solid-looking football rolling idly towards him. He looked up slightly, and there was a pair of heavy boots, strong legs, baggy shorts and a red and blue shirt.

'Isn't this a stroke of luck?' said William.

Maybe, thought Chris instantly. But who for?

Fourteen

'William! Hi!'

'I'm so glad you came. I've really been looking forward to this.'

'You have?' Chris enquired, trying to pull himself together.

'Yes! Come on.'

William's face seemed quite calm, given that he had caught Chris coming out of his squat (was there any other explanation?), holding one of his candles. He just turned and walked towards the cleared waste ground beyond the end of the street. When Chris didn't follow him automatically, he looked back, actually managing to appear even more confused than Chris was himself.

'Aren't you coming?'

'Coming where?'

'To practise! I thought you wanted to work on your tackling.'

Chris was speechless. He didn't dare move either.

'Come on! The ground's better over here.'

Chris still hesitated. Fleeing wasn't an option because of the fences blocking off access to the main road. He stood up, picking up his bag in his left hand. William smiled, clearly satisfied that Chris was finally getting his act together. Almost.

'Chris . . .'

Chris halted, almost frozen once again. 'What?'

'Bring the ball.'

William set off again and Chris followed, some distance behind, his bag gripped tight in one fist and the ball at his feet. They marched past the fire on to a clear and level patch of ground.

William beckoned to Chris to knock the ball over, and took the pass on his upper instep, flicking the ball up so that he could trap it on his chest. When it fell to the ground again, he killed it dead with one touch.

'Where's your kit?' he asked.

'I – uh . . .' Chris managed by way of explanation.

William looked disappointed, but shrugged and chipped the ball back towards Chris with an effortless swing.

'I suppose it doesn't matter,' he said. 'Come on, let's see what you can do. Knock a few passes over.'

There were questions, comments, ideas and fears queuing up in Chris's brain, looking for a way to get themselves spoken. He couldn't even begin to organise the way he felt about the situation. Standing up, he took that first pass from William on the inside of his foot, knocked it clear of his bag, then stabbed a flat pass to William's feet. They exchanged passes rapidly, moving out into the clear space. Chris knew he was buying time, sheltering behind the one thing he knew he could control – the ball. William was obviously impressed at the accuracy of the passes he received, since he moved further back each time. He hit his own returns back with increasing power. Chris brought each one under control first time until the last.

Reaching for one that was just a little wider, Chris stretched out his arms for balance and immediately his right elbow reminded him that he was supposed to be resting it. William saw Chris wince with pain.

'You OK?'

'It's nothing,' replied Chris quickly. He bit his lip and stroked the ball back. William trapped it with the sole of his boot and let it rest there.

'Are you sure?'

'I just stepped on something a bit awkwardly,' Chris insisted. He kicked a fragment of brick away across the ground. 'This isn't exactly a perfect surface, you know.'

William laughed. 'Do you always play on a nice flat piece of grass?'

Chris thought of the surface of the pitch the Colts used for home games; while not exactly lush, it did at least have some grass on it, and there weren't small piles of earth all over the place, waiting to turn over an ankle.

'Sometimes,' was his answer.

William looked around. 'Not me. I learned to play on the street outside my front door. Me and some mates would pretend to be Oldcester United, and we'd play against one of the other streets, who'd be Arsenal or Wolves . . .'

'Didn't they want to be United too?' asked Chris, as intrigued as always when William allowed a glimpse into his past.

'Of course – but our street was closest to the ground. We had first choice.'

Chris digested that piece of logic quickly. He was keen to get on to meatier things.

'When was that?' asked Chris, hoping William would answer a direct question for a change.

'When I was about six or seven,' William replied, his expression distant as he recalled those (long?) distant days. Chris wondered what he would see, if he was able to look through William's memory. Or through his imagination.

William's face clouded over suddenly. 'But then Jack Schwarz arrived, and everything changed. Older than me, you see. Thought he could play a bit. He took over the game, froze me out. It got to the point where we were fighting more than we were playing.'

'Why didn't he like you?' asked Chris.

'Because I was better than he was and he knew it. He could never catch me, on the field or off.'

The anger and frustration on William's face was vivid. Chris wondered exactly what had gone on between the two of them, to turn two neighbours into such bitter enemies.

'He played for United before I did. They didn't reckon much to him, though. I could have told them the same myself! He played a couple of games, then they dropped him into the reserves. When I came into the side, he was furious. Said he'd make sure I was thrown out, that kind of thing.'

'And did he?'

William put on a wry smile. 'He tried. It never came to much, not at first. There wasn't time for much mischief.' With that, he looked up at Chris. 'Speaking of which, if we're going to get anything done, we'd best be on with it! You'll be late home!'

'I'm already well past late,' Chris muttered to himself, but he made no attempt to leave. He wanted to hear more about William and Jack Schwarz; more about William playing for Oldcester. Not ten minutes before, Chris had been quite prepared to believe that William was nothing more or less than a squatter living in a ruined house. Now, once again, he found himself caught up in William's story. True or false, Chris wanted to hear more. He couldn't leave.

William was through talking for now, though. He collected the ball from Chris, rolling it back and forth under his foot.

'So, what do you want to work on? Tackling?'

Chris had changed his mind about that as well. 'The other day,' he said, 'in the park. You took the ball off me really easily. I've always thought I could run with the ball pretty well, but you made me look easy to tackle.'

'Ah!' said William, smiling. 'Well, I told you I was a pretty good defender. And you tend to let the ball run a way ahead of you . . . you need to keep it closer.'

Without another word spoken, except for William explaining technique to Chris and directing him how to run with the ball, they slipped into a simple exercise, with Chris running back and forth between two of the more pronounced piles of rubble while William patrolled the space, trying to prevent Chris's passage. They played slowly at first, as William encouraged Chris to keep the ball closer. Gradually, though, they upped the pace, until Chris was sprinting as fast as he could between the two piles, swerving this way and that to avoid William's challenges. Sometimes, he even managed it.

'Stay balanced!' William shouted. 'Use your arms!'

Ignoring the pain as best he could, Chris tried to follow William's lead. Bit by bit, he could feel it becoming more natural to steer the ball by gentler, more frequent touches, rather than knocking it forward and haring after it. Changing direction became more fluid. Twice, he left William tackling fresh air.

'That's it!' William laughed, then he closed in on Chris again. 'Small touches; try to feint one way, then the other. Step over the ball sometimes — it'll make the defender think you're about to turn when you're not. Try to keep your body between him and the ball.'

Chris listened and tried to put the ideas into practice. It was only when he nutmegged William that he came to grief, colliding with his playing partner and crashing to the ground. He wrenched himself round as he fell, trying to avoid landing on his injured arm, which only made the fall itself worse.

'Are you all right?' cried William, rushing over. Chris sat up, holding his elbow. The jarring impact had caused a jolt of pain to lance through the elbow, almost as bad as when he first hurt it.

'I've a bit of a crook elbow, that's all,' Chris grunted, biting his lip as he waited for the pain to go away. 'I've got some pain-killers in my bag.'

'Medicine?' asked William. 'I'll get it.'

William raced over to where they had left the bag and dived in. Rummaging around, he immediately discovered the tin Chris had found under the stairs in the house. Chris noticed his face cloud over once again. There was a long delay before William put the tin on the ground and pulled out Chris's jacket, searching in the pockets until he found the small white tub.

'Is this the stuff?' William asked. His voice sounded tense.

Chris nodded. William walked back and handed him the jar. Chris took two of the pain-killers, wishing he had something to wash them down with.

Even before the worst of the pain (and the disgusting taste of the pills, which was almost worse) had started to die down, William hauled Chris to his feet by his good arm. He handed Chris the sling.

'If you were hurt, you shouldn't have played.'

'I wanted to,' said Chris. 'You've really showed me a lot. I –'

'Too much, I think,' William interrupted, appearing dark and serious. 'Certainly enough for today. I have to be going now.'

'Where?' asked Chris, but William's face told him there would be no more questions answered today. The older man was looking around, shivering slightly as if he had just noticed that the evening was too cool to be running around in just a football shirt. He started to move away.

'Are we going to practise again?' asked Chris. William didn't answer. 'Wait!' Chris called after him. 'I'll walk out with you. I have to ask you something!' The gap was still growing. Chris ran towards his bag, which only opened a wider space between them.

That was when he noticed a blue light, flashing off the face of the buildings in Warwick Street.

'Someone's noticed that little fire I made,' Chris said as he picked up his bag. There was no answer. He looked round quickly, but William had disappeared.

They were 40 metres from the end of the terraces of Coventry Street. There was no way William could have gone past Chris that way. There were a few high piles of rubble towards the railway lines, but surely nothing that could have hidden William so completely from view.

But he was gone. Like smoke . . . or like a ghost.

There was no time to search. Chris only knew one way out, through the opening in the fence on Coventry Street. He had to get there before the police found any other way in, or sealed off that one. He ran quickly towards the houses, looking back just once at the small, bare patch of earth they had been playing on, wondering if any of the old United ground lay underneath. There was no-one in sight, but Chris still fancied he could hear the sound of a crowd cheering in the wind.

It took him an hour to realise he still had the ball.

'There isn't going to be a discussion about this,' Chris's father said, almost throwing the plate of hurriedly cooked pizza on to the counter. 'You're grounded. You don't go to school tomorrow. You stay here all day, and you stay in every day this week. I'll call from work. If you don't answer . . . then God help you.'

Chris had never seen his father this angry before. He tried to take a mouthful of the food, but it tasted of ashes and despair. He was starving too. He took a look at the clock on the kitchen wall. It was 9.35; he had been in fifteen minutes.

His father was right about there being no discussion. Chris had uttered an 'I'm sorry' during the last fifteen minutes and that was about it. He was trying to decide what would sound worse – silence or the truth. The truth boiled down to the fact that he and Nicky had been into the city together, which was OK, but that Nicky had been home about seven (which was more borderline) while Chris had stayed out until gone nine looking for a ghost on a building site.

Silence, then.

The phone rang. His father went to answer it.

'Hello,' he barked into the receiver, as if it were due a grounding as well. 'Nicky? No, you can't. Yes, he's back, but you can't speak to him. Because he's taken a vow of silence. Oh, and Nicky; he's not going to be in school tomorrow, and he won't be leaving the house at all until Saturday. Don't call; don't come round.'

With that, Mr Stephens put the phone down. He looked at Chris through the kitchen door and pointed at the instrument as if it had just appeared by magic.

'Will you look at that?' he stormed, his voice loud and sarcastic. 'You can talk to people from a long way away with this thing! Amazing! Just think, if you were staying out late, you'd be able to tell someone!'

Chris took the point. He didn't mention that the houses on Warwick Street had probably been disconnected. However, he did feel he ought to stick up for his mate.

'Don't take it out on Nicky. It isn't his fault.'

'Don't worry; Fiorentini has problems of his own, without needing any of yours. Apparently he came home covered in some grease, and let slip he'd been chased by a security guard. Were you still together at that point in the evening's entertainment, or do I have a different story to look forward to?'

Nice one, Nicky.

'It wasn't anything. Some guy in a uniform made a mistake. It all got sorted out. We didn't do anything.'

Chris knew his father wasn't happy with that non-explanation. Trying to hide the whole truth wasn't going to make things any better. Even so, Chris couldn't see any way he could explain what he had been doing up at Star Park without convincing his father that he had lost his mind completely.

'Eat,' Mr Stephens commanded, leaving Chris to it. 'I don't want a second dinner to go to waste.' He went back out of the kitchen and into the living room. Chris heard the TV behind the closed door.

As soon as he had finished the makeshift meal, Chris went up to his room. He realised that he had left his bag downstairs, but decided not to go back and get it. He was in bed before 10.30. Nothing else had been said.

The dull throbbing in his arm was slowly fading. The ache in his guts was not. Things hadn't turned out the way he'd planned at all.

Fifteen

His father had gone to work before Chris made an appearance the following morning. Chris knew that this meant his dad hadn't yet calmed down.

Chris went to the phone. He had no intention of defying his father, but there was no way he could let things remain as they were. He dialled the number from memory.

As soon as he heard a voice at the other end, he whispered: 'Jazz?' He realised in the same instant whispering was pretty pointless, but that didn't make him stop. 'It's me, Chris.'

'Hey! What happened to you last ni–' Jazz began, his voice muffled as if he had a mouthful of breakfast.

'Jazz,' Chris said, cutting his friend off. 'I need you to do something.'

'Hang on!' cried Jazz, interrupting Chris in turn. 'Don't you want to hear what we found out yesterday? You won't believe it!'

'It'll have to wait. You have to get to school and I shouldn't be talking. So listen. After school, get everyone round at your place or Mac's, and call me from there. You can give me this amazing news then.'

'How come?' asked Jazz, who liked life to be straightforward. 'I thought we'd be able to talk about things at break.'

'I won't be in school today.'

Jazz's tone changed to one of concern. 'What's the matter?'

'I'll tell you later. Just get things sorted the way I said, OK? Tell Nicky he mustn't phone me; it has to be you or Mac. Do you understand?'

He very much doubted that Jazz did, but he got an affirmative answer and then rang off. He was in no mood to have to explain the situation to Jazz this morning and then reel it all off again to the others as they called one by one. Besides, this way he didn't break his father's instructions, which only specified not going out, and not making or receiving calls from Nicky. If Nicky was at someone else's house when they called, that didn't count, right?

Having settled things so that he could keep up with developments in the William mystery without having broken any of his father's rules (well, not by too much, anyway), Chris made himself some breakfast and read the newspaper. There were no startling developments in the Virgin/Oldcester United story, so the paper was forced to give the whole back page over to some cricket. Some commentator was suggesting that England's next winter tour would probably be to Iceland, and that they'd still lose all five tests even then.

There was only so much entertainment to be gained from reading the rest of the paper, which was so pressed for real news that it was forced to print two stories that were little more than rumours, one suggesting that Take That were about to reform and another that *Casualty* and *EastEnders* were going to be merged into one soap.

There was even less entertainment to be had watching daytime TV, so Chris went upstairs to log on to his computer. A few months before, he and some other fans had put together a home page for Oldcester United, and Chris liked to keep up to date with how it had developed. Chris didn't stop to consider if his father's restriction on using the phone covered connecting to CompuServe.

Today, though, the club's Web site wasn't much more interesting than the newspaper Chris had abandoned. It too was full of rumour. A few people had got hold of the story that United were about to splash out on a new striker, possibly Dwight Yorke, or that they were signing a young lad from Kenya to play in goal. Chris left a message for anyone who knew anything about United's history before World War One to e-mail him.

Twenty minutes later, he logged off, mindful that his father might try to call. Within seconds, the phone rang. Chris ran downstairs and picked it up.

'Hello?'

'What did I say about using the phone?'

Chris decided against answering that directly, in case he managed to trap himself. 'Dad, I was using the computer!'

'Well, don't. If you want to log on, do it tonight when I get home. I don't want to call again later and get another busy signal.'

The line went dead. This was a reasonably clear sign that the grounding was still in force.

Chris replaced the receiver, sighing. It was going to be a long day. The only consolation was that he didn't appear to have made his arm any worse playing around with William. In fact, it felt –

Chris realised he was looking at his bag, still where he had dropped it the night before. He stepped over and unzipped it. It was still there – the ball they had been playing with on the waste ground. It was a Mitre, almost brand new. It felt solid, not at all ghostly. Shouldn't it be dripping ectoplasm, or whatever it was they called that drooly, oily green gunk that's always used in ghost films?

So, what did that mean, in the greater scheme of things? Could ghosts wander into sports stores to buy footballs? Or had William just happened across it somewhere? Chris thought about this one piece of solid evidence for a while. Perhaps it proved that Nicky was right all along.

He'd have to take it back to William sometime, just as soon as the grounding was over. Wondering just how long that might be, Chris dropped the ball back into the bag.

It hit the old tin with a solid clank.

The sound reminded Chris very forcefully of his exploration of the house in Warwick Street. All kinds of thoughts flooded into his brain; how there was an A–Z of Oldcester in the dining room, which would clear up the business of whether the unmarked road had been Warwick Street; how he hadn't managed to get back upstairs in the house to record the names written on the wall, and how he'd have to persuade Nicky or one of the others to go; and of how strange he had felt when he had realised the cellar door was ajar.

It was as if someone had wanted him to find the book that lay inside the tin. But who? William had looked quite surprised and disappointed when he had found it in Chris's bag, and had gone off in virtual silence thereafter.

Chris had been suffering too much discomfort on the bus to read it on the way back last night, and then he had walked into the row with his father. Nothing was stopping him now.

Jack Schwarz's voice rang out from the stand like a church bell on a clear, calm day. Even over the massed voices of the thousands packed into the stand, it stood out like a doleful funeral chime. Billy recognised it at once.

It was the death of all his hopes.

'Mr Forbes! Mr Forbes, sir!'

The United manager was just as quick to identify the caller's voice. His heavy brow lowered in a deep frown as he turned round, locating the source of that urgent summons straight away.

Jack was in the crowd. Not even among the reserve team players clustered behind the bench on which Mr Forbes had occasionally parked his ample behind during the course of the first half. In the crowd. Somehow, he had pushed his way through the press to the edge of the stand, overlooking the area on the halfway line from where those attending the two teams were watching the game. Others were turning to see who was yelling at the United manager, wondering who had the nerve. They all knew Jack.

'Mr Forbes!'

'Be quiet, lad!' the manager admonished Schwarz. 'What are you doing here?'

'Come to see the game, sir!' explained Jack, beaming.

He looked very pleased with himself. Billy felt a cold dread hand clutching at his guts. Anything that pleased Jack Schwarz could only mean trouble for Billy Murdoch.

'So watch it, lad. You might learn something.'

'I shall sir, I shall!' Schwarz grinned, full of himself. He was bobbing up and down with excitement. Mr Forbes gave him a long glare and prepared to turn away to give his attention to the game once more.

'Mr Forbes, sir!' Jack called, his voice pitched higher and louder than before. 'Shall you put Billy Murdoch on at half-time, sir?'

Mr Forbes turned around again, his heavy body slow and stiff.

The dark eyes, just under the brim of his bowler hat, were black with rage.

'What's that to do with you, Mr Schwarz?' he growled. He pronounced the name with thick anger. Some of the men in the crowd, attracted to the growing row, hissed.

Jack ignored them. His whole being was focused on the mischief he was making.

'You'll recall, Mr Forbes, sir, how I told you Billy Murdoch was a liar and a thief, who'd blacken the name of this club if he wore its shirt?'

Forbes's moustache twitched. It was clear he never forgot anything.

'Aye! And I told you then, Mr Schwarz, as I'll tell you now. If you have any proof, produce it! If not, hold your tongue! I dropped you from the team because of your mischief-making. Don't make me have you ejected from the ground for the same reason!'

Billy watched all this with growing dread, knowing that many of the faces which had been turned to face first Schwarz and then Mr Forbes were now shifted in his direction, trying to see what his response would be. Billy gave them nothing to work with but a look of pure horror. Jack must have known how Mr Forbes would react. Something must be giving him the confidence to face United's stern, uncompromising boss.

Billy didn't have long to wait to find out what that was.

'But I have proof, Mr Forbes! Aye, and I've the police here an' all, come to take Billy Murdoch into custody! My father told them how Billy's been stealing from our stall in the market since he were a boy, and about how he were there again this morning, taking fruit when he thought no-one were looking. But there were a witness this time . . .'

The triumphant glint in Schwarz's eyes grew even brighter. For the first time since he had first called out, he looked directly at Billy.

'I've got you this time, Billy! You're fixed, good and proper!'

Billy got up on to his feet, fists clenched at his side, crouched ready to spring at his accuser. His face was flushed with shame and fury. Of all days for this to happen . . .

He could hear Mr Forbes behind him, moving closer. He could sense the outstretched arm reaching for his shoulder.

'Billy, lad . . .' the gruff voice came, trying so hard to be gentle.

Billy didn't wait to hear the next words. What could Mr Forbes say? Would he ask if Schwarz was telling the truth? Would he ask if Billy had ever stolen from the Schwarz stall in the market at the end of the White Hill Road? And what could Billy say in reply?

Because, at the bottom of the pile, the accusation was true.

Ever since the first day that Jack Schwarz had come to live in Coventry Street, like a dark cloud over the good days that had gone before, Billy had lived in fear of Jack's angry fists. Quickly, everyone had turned against him. All of his friends had seen that Jack would never accept Billy as being better at football than him, and that he would crush anyone who said that it was true. To survive, all the other boys had sided with Jack, sheltering behind his hatred of Billy.

Billy had been left alone. His father had died in the same year as the old queen, so there had been no-one to help him. His mother tried hard to make a living for them both, but work was hard to find and the Schwarz family — father, uncles, and sons — did all they could to make it harder.

So, from the time he was eight, Billy had fought back the only way he knew how. He and his mother had to eat, so he stole. Since it was the Schwarz clan which kept them from having jam on the table, he stole from them.

It only made things worse between him and Jack, of course, but Billy didn't mind. Jack was older, and bigger, but he didn't have Billy's nimble mind or his desperate courage. The same skills and attitude that made Billy a better footballer also enabled him to outwit Jack in every other 'game' they played.

Each defeat only made Jack even more determined to find a way to destroy Billy in the end. Standing there, on the touchline, with a hundred eyes on him from the crowd, with his team mates watching in amazement, with Mr Forbes reaching out for him, Billy knew that the end had come.

He screamed out, then leapt across towards the wall of the stand. Jack was surprised, of course, but he had time to recover and flinch back as Billy came at him. He fell back into the crowd like a swimmer disappearing under water. Billy clutched at thin air as the crowd flowed into the space Jack left behind.

He waited for a few seconds, hoping that Jack would reappear. When he did, his arch-enemy was several yards back in the crowd, surrounded by confused men looking this way and that, trying to make sense of what was going on around them. There was no way Billy could reach him.

And what good would it have done if he had?

He looked back, and saw Mr Forbes looking at him with his dark, steady gaze. He knew the United manager had taken his actions as a sure sign of guilt. Why else would Billy have acted the way he did?

There was a narrow passage through the stand that led to the changing rooms and the Warwick Street exit. Billy felt a stab of fear in his heart. If the police were coming, he might have only a few seconds to escape. He had to move now!

Without another glance back, he took off, sprinting headlong down the tunnel. He heard the gasp of the crowd and players as they realised – or thought they realised – just what it was they had witnessed. The fugitive was fleeing before the law could catch up with him.

Billy went out through the gates at top speed, his boots clattering on the cobbled roadway. He didn't even pause at his home. He just took off, leaving his dreams behind him.

The last thing he heard as he left the ground was the plaintive wail of a locomotive whistle and the thunderous rumble as a munitions train left the marshalling yard, heading south for the coast and the growing conflict. He thought about what Mr Forbes had said; about how he had to take his chance while he could. Billy knew that war had been declared on Germany and her allies and that the British Expeditionary Force was already in France, preparing to stand shoulder to shoulder with the French army against the Hun.

Jack had snatched Billy's chance of one kind of glory from him. Perhaps there was another opportunity waiting for him in Flanders . . .

Chris put the old book down on the counter and took a deep breath. His mouth was dry. He crossed to the sink and drew a tall glass of fresh, cool water.

As he drank it in long, steady gulps, he tried to straighten out his mind. He had no doubt about what he had just read, but even so it amazed him. He looked up at the clock and realised it was already gone two o'clock. It had been slow, hard work getting through the book. Each page was as fragile as an autumn leaf, brittle and yellow with age. Some had pieces missing. On all of them, the ink was faded almost to the point of being unreadable.

Yet piece by piece, Chris had managed to decipher each line, working his way through the cramped, spidery handwriting that covered each page. It didn't all make sense, but Chris found that each fragment helped him see more of the whole picture. The more he read, the more he understood.

It wasn't exactly a diary, but it seemed to record events in the order they had happened, from the early stories about playing football in the street with friends, to the arrival of Jack Schwarz and the dark shadow he cast, to that fateful day when Billy Murdoch's hopes and dreams had been shattered in the most cruel way. All that, in just the first third of the book.

There was no name on the cover or the title page, but Chris knew what he had found – and he thought he knew why William had looked so downcast when he discovered Chris had taken it from the house on Warwick Street.

This was William's book. This was William's life.

At some point, for reasons Chris doubted that he would ever understand, William had decided to write down the story of his life. He hadn't included every detail – there was nothing in the book about life at school, or what had happened to his father, just that he had died when William was quite young – but he had concentrated on the issues that mattered most to him. Which came down to football and Jack Schwarz. The light and the dark.

After a while, Chris realised he wasn't just reading the bare words; he was almost being transported back all those years to stand in Warwick Street when its two rows of small terraced houses were populated with the young families of railway workers. He could hear the steam trains pulling out of Oldcester's main railway station, heading north past the old depot which had been transformed in 40 years from bare earth to a ramshackle stadium which could hold 42,000 fans, packed in like sardines. On match days, Warwick Street would be filled with men in dark suits and flat caps, queuing at the turnstiles to watch United, the team which had started off as a spare-time activity for railwaymen, but which had become the sporting soul of the growing city.

Chris imagined what it must have seemed like to young William Murdoch, watching all those men outside his front window on Saturdays, then going out in the week to play on that same street, in the shadow of the stands that blocked the late afternoon sun from the front of his house.

When he realised he had talent, what else could William dream about except that one day those same queues of men would be standing in line outside the house where he was born, waiting to buy their ticket and see him run out on to the field in United's red and blue? Every word he read convinced Chris that William had never really thought of doing anything else in his life but play football. It was the only thing worth living for.

That's why I can't get William out of my head, Chris thought. He's just like me.

The telephone's shrill warble disrupted that line of thinking. Chris picked it up smartly, convinced it was his father.

'What's all this about?' demanded Nicky.

Chris sighed. So much for his attempt to keep within the boundaries his father had set. He quickly explained the situation to Nicky.

'Oh, right,' said Nicky, and he rang off.

Chris was left holding the receiver, utterly amazed. As soon as he put it down, it rang again.

'It's me,' said Mac.

'Hi,' said Chris, preparing to start the explanation all over again.

'Nicky just told us. That's why I'm ringing back.' He told Chris they had got out of school early. The summer holidays had officially begun. Chris gradually cottoned on to what was happening. Nicky, Jazz and Russell were all at Mac's. Apparently Jazz hadn't got the message across at school, so Nicky had dialled first. Now they were going along with Chris's plan – he wasn't speaking to Nicky, he was speaking to Mac, so it would be all right with his father.

'What none of us understand is why you were so late home,' Mac continued. 'Nicky must have beat you back by hours.'

Chris launched into the next part of the story. He told Mac about realising that William had been talking about the old

123

Star Park, the one by the railway, when he said its shadow fell on his house. He told him about the way the area was being demolished, and about how he had found William's house.

'That'll be why he came back,' Chris heard Jazz say. Mac must have been holding the phone so that the other three could hear it. 'His old home being knocked down has brought him back from limbo.'

'If that was the case,' Nicky snorted, 'the world would be crawling with ghosts. Every house that got knocked down, there'd be another dozen of them running around wanting to play football with Chris.'

Chris heard the others laughing.

'Sounds to me like this William is squatting there,' said Russell, who wasn't a very superstitious person either.

'That's what I thought at first,' said Chris, 'but wait until you hear what I found next.' He told them about the drawings and writing on the wall, marks that must have been covered by wallpaper for years until the last occupant moved out and the house started to decay.

'We could check those names against team lists from 1914,' Jazz said, excitedly. 'That would prove William was alive then!'

'How?' scoffed Nicky. 'Anyone could have found those names and written them on the wall. It could just be a wind-up.' Chris knew that this was true, but what would be the point? It would have taken a lot of work to research the names – look at the trouble they had had. And how was the writer to know that Chris or anyone else would find them and know what they were? It didn't seem possible that it could be a hoax.

'Maybe not,' said Russell, 'but there's another explanation. Someone was squatting in that house, we know that for sure. Suppose it's William – a real flesh and blood bloke. Say he's a bit disturbed, and started thinking he was someone else. He might have adopted William Murdoch's identity, started pretending he was William Murdoch when he's really some-one else.'

It was possible. Russell could even supply a name.

'Mac and I checked round Memorial Park yesterday. No sign of William, of course. Then we went round the back of the park and we found this home, a kind of rehabilitation centre for kids and young men and women who've had drug problems or whatever. We got chatting to this social worker there. Apparently, several of the guys like to hang round the park.'

'So?'

'So, we told this woman that we'd seen a guy in an old United football shirt over the park. We said how we'd lost something, and that he might have taken it. She said they'd had this guy in named David Kirke, who had all kinds of emotional problems. He'd gone missing the week before. She said he was crazy about football, and told people he'd played for Manchester United.'

It was clear that Russell had decided that Kirke and William were the same person. Mac, who'd been happy to believe in the ghost theory before, was almost convinced as well.

'It really does sound like this is your guy, Chris,' he said.

Chris was sure that if he thought hard enough, he'd be able to come up with dozens of reasons why Kirke couldn't be William. It was just that he couldn't think of any right then. He decided to move on to the next part of the story.

'OK, listen. I went to find some paper to write down the names, and he was there.'

'Who?'

'William! Who did you think? He had a ball with him and we went off to practise passing and dribbling, just like we'd said.'

'You said he was going to teach you tackling,' said Nicky, sourly. Chris felt his frustration starting to boil up. Nicky was missing the point.

'He was there! In Warwick Street! If he was your Kirke guy, don't you think it would be a bit of a coincidence, turning up like that? Just where I expected to find William?'

That silenced the others, except for Mac who offered a whispered, 'Cool!'

'I haven't even got to the best part yet,' said Chris. 'We practised, and he was really good. I mean, he showed me a lot, you know? There's no doubt in my mind that he's good enough to have been a United player.'

'Where did the ball come from?' asked Nicky, which was the same question that had niggled Chris about the encounter too.

'Does it matter?'

'It's just that if Kirke was pretending to be William Murdoch,' said Russell, once again displaying cool, reasoned logic (it was really starting to get on Chris's nerves), 'then he could easily have found out about William living in Warwick Street, or he could have gone there just because it was close to the old ground. It's not a coincidence you keep bumping into him – you're both chasing after the same thing, from different ends.'

'So it was Kirke's ball?' asked Mac, veering back towards the other side again. Russell must have nodded or something at the other end because there was a brief silence and then Mac added: 'That makes sense.'

It was time to play the ace.

'OK, what about this? I found a book.'

'A book?' they all cried together.

'What kind of book?' Nicky added.

Chris told them what he had found and what he had read that morning. It took him several minutes. The other four listened in silence as he told them William's story up to the point where he had fled from the ground after Jack's accusation.

'Wow!' Mac sighed. Chris heard Jazz say something too, to which Nicky offered a mocking reply.

'What?' Chris demanded.

'Chris, there was no football in 1914. The First World War started, remember?'

Chris remembered the facts well enough (although he was amazed that Nicky did – Nicky hated history almost as much as he hated geography). Some Austrian duke got killed in Sarajevo, which was in Bosnia. All the major powers had ended up at war as a result, including Britain, who had sided with France and Russia against Germany and Austria.

'The war had only just started,' Chris insisted. 'Maybe they didn't cancel the football season straight away. And besides, this was only a friendly. It might have been played anyway.'

'It still doesn't prove anything, Chris,' Russell began patiently.

'Oh, no! Not this time!' Chris yelled. 'This isn't something your Kirke bloke could have written. This is old. The book's almost falling to pieces. It must have been down in that cellar for years!'

'Does it say what happened to William?' Mac asked, innocently.

'You mean does it say "I died yesterday"?' scoffed Nicky. 'Get real!'

Chris gently turned to the last page on which there was any writing. It was harder to read this page than any of the others. Chris worked out that it was talking about the war, and how disgusting it was living in the trenches. It didn't end in any dramatic way; the last sentence just mentioned that William was due some leave in a few days' time. After that there were just blank pages.

'I'm not sure that helps us at all,' said Nicky, blandly. Chris could picture him looking grumpy and flicking back his hair.

'Doesn't help?! Doesn't *help*?! It's William's story! It's proof! When you take all the pieces, it shows that he has to be real, doesn't it?'

'Real . . . as in a ghost?' asked Jazz.

'Yes! You just have to put it all together and –'

'I've got it,' said Russell. 'I see it now.'

Chris was almost ready to scream with joy. If he'd persuaded Russell . . .

'We've had this the wrong way round. Kirke left the home *before* he saw Chris that first time, right? He must have moved into the squat and found the book. I bet it was in the cellar, hidden away somewhere. No-one who'd ever lived there since the war had ever found it, but now the place was completely empty Kirke must have discovered it somehow and read it. That's when he started believing he was William Murdoch.'

'No!' cried Chris unhappily, but a small part of his mind was already saying, yes, that's it. There was no ghost, just a sad, lonely guy whose own life was such a mess he had started pretending to be someone else. Chris slid down the hall wall, squatting on his haunches while he tried to think of some way that he could counter Russell's argument. Nothing came to mind.

'It's still interesting, though,' Russell was saying. 'The book's real. I bet the club would love to have it – you know how little stuff they have from that far back. We could find out some more about William, and give it all to them.'

'Do you want to hear what I found?' asked Jazz. Chris remained silent, but the others were still enjoying the adventure and urged Jazz to reveal his piece of the puzzle.

'OK, I discovered two brilliant bits in the library. First, there was all this stuff about the Oldcester Old Pals.'

'The who?' asked Nicky.

'They were a regiment in the army, formed here in Old-cester right at the start of World War One. All volunteers. Men were rushing to join up after war was declared in August. It says about some of the railwaymen joining up, but the government didn't want too many of them leaving their jobs, because the railways had to be kept running.'

'What, if you were a station porter you didn't have to fight?' asked Nicky.

Jazz sighed, and explained that he was talking more about drivers and skilled engineers. 'OK, now get this. I made a photocopy of the list of people who joined the Oldcester Old Pals at the beginning of the war.' Chris heard the rustle of paper as Jazz leafed through the list. 'Then we compared it with the names you guys found in Mr Lively's office. William Murdoch wasn't on the Old Pals list – nor was Jack Schwarz. But there was a Jack Swain.'

'Swain? But that was the name of the guy who was putting together United's history . . .'

'That's what Nicky said. I remembered it because I saw Jack Swain when I was looking for Schwarz. That's when it struck me. I remember reading that lots of people who had German-sounding names changed them when the war broke out. The ones that didn't had their windows broken, that kind of thing. So I wondered . . .'

'You think Jack Schwarz joined these Old Pals using a fake name?'

'Not a fake name, Nicky. A new name. It's just easier if you sound English. It's like you guys all call me Jazz. My real name is Javinder. It doesn't bother me that you don't use it – I've grown used to Jazz. Maybe, one day, I'll decide that Jazz is a better name to live with, even at work and stuff.'

'You can actually change your legal name,' Mac added. 'There's some agency or something the government runs. You write to them, pay them about fifty quid, and you can call yourself what you like.'

'OK, so William didn't join the Old Pals but this Jack guy may have done,' Nicky summarised. 'So?'

'Well, then there's the second thing I found. That war memorial in the park? I found a full list of all the names on it.'

'And?' Nicky demanded once Jazz paused. Chris knew how much Nicky hated to be spoon-fed information. Even though, on this occasion, he must have heard all this before, he was still urging Jazz to cut to the chase.

'And this time it's the other way round. No Swain, but William Murdoch is on it. He was killed in 1915, just after New Year, serving with the Sherwood Regiment. He was just sixteen years old. When he joined up, he wasn't much more than fifteen.'

That gave them all something to think about. Chris was still crouched against the wall, the phone held against his ear. He couldn't quite come to terms with everything he was hearing. The things that Jazz had discovered tied in so well with what they knew about William. But what did it matter? Millions had died in the First World War – the only thing that had made William special was that he had come back.

Only now, it appeared, he hadn't.

'Chris?' Nicky's voice was full of concern.

'Still here,' Chris announced. His voice sounded ragged with emotion.

'Look, just because the ghost thing didn't work out, it doesn't mean this has all been a waste of time. Russell's right. We should collect all the evidence together and give it to the club. Maybe the newspaper.'

'I'll take a camera out there and get a picture of the wall,' said Mac.

'And we could still go to see this Swain guy, and find out what he knows,' Nicky continued.

'Yeah,' said Chris. 'Maybe.' He suddenly felt very tired. 'Listen, I have to go. My father might be trying to get through.'

'Sure – understood,' replied Nicky. 'We'll –'

Chris didn't hear the rest. He put the phone down.

The book was on the floor between his feet. He picked it up and put it back in the tin. After a few seconds of looking at it, he left it there, replaced the lid and went to make himself some lunch.

Sixteen

When his father got home, he explained everything. It took quite a while. Sandwiched in the middle, there was a visit to the doctor who said that he was confident Chris would feel no ill effect from the injury by Saturday.

Chris felt better. He realised that the injury had been niggling at his mind over the last day or two. He hadn't enjoyed rowing with his father, either. He would be happy to put both incidents behind him.

Satisfied that he understood what had been going on and that Chris was cured of his brief bout of insanity, Mr Stephens lifted the grounding. Even so, Chris didn't much feel like going out during the day on Wednesday. Mac had called up just after midday. As promised, he'd been to Warwick Street to take a picture of the wall only to find that the last few houses were being demolished. In addition, Jazz had been back at the library, where a woman had said that someone else had been looking through the same books and records he'd asked for. Jazz believed it was Kirke.

By the evening, however, Chris was in a better mood. Wednesday night was the night for training with the Colts. Chris repacked his bag with his football kit and went off to join the others.

The book stayed behind, in the drawer of his computer table.

Chris had no intention of doing any strenuous training – he wanted his arm to heal up properly – but he hated being inactive, so a few exercises and drills under the watchful eye of Iain Walsh seemed to be just what the doctor might have ordered.

As he stepped out of the front door, he could feel a change

in the air. The forecast was for some patchy fog to appear in the evening, with rain to follow before dawn. After the few warm days earlier in the week, this was a return to the changeable weather of the last few weeks of term, when summer seemed months away. Chris took one look at the clouds overhead and went back inside for his baseball jacket.

It didn't take very long to walk from his home to the university campus sports field, which was the Colts' home base. There was an all-weather pitch there, and an excellent grass field. The changing facilities had been a little less than perfect since a fire had razed the old cricket pavilion to the ground, but some temporary cabins were in place on the car park. There was talk that the pavilion might be rebuilt in the autumn, thanks to a Lottery grant.

Several of the rest of the team were there already, including Jazz, the captain, Zak, and Chris's striking partner, Rory Blackstone. Iain hadn't arrived yet, but it wasn't unusual for him to be a few minutes late.

As he stepped through the gates, Chris noticed that there was a little low mist already on the ground, particularly nearer the river.

He walked along the drive, then cut across the grass to where the others were warming up. They were a little surprised to see him — obviously word of the injury had filtered round the group.

It wasn't the only thing that they had been talking about.

'Hey — it's Egon!' called Polly.

'Sorry?' Chris responded, bemused.

'Who you gonna call?!' Polly cackled, and he and the others burst into the theme from *Ghostbusters*.

Chris shot Jazz a murderous look which the midfielder quickly avoided by pretending he needed to relace his trainers.

'Very funny,' sighed Chris as the chorus came to an end.

'No, really,' laughed Stamp, 'did you really think this William bloke was a ghost?'

Chris wasn't going to dignify this with an answer but Jazz looked up, obviously determined to make amends.

'It really did seem a bit odd at first . . .' he offered. When he caught sight of Chris's expression, he decided to check out his other foot.

The Colts' left back, Tollie, arrived at about the same time, which was a cue for everyone to start the same joke again, singing even louder. Chris marched off towards the porta-cabin, only to find it was locked. Of course, Walsh hadn't arrived yet . . .

'Perhaps you could just go through the wall,' called Polly. The others fell about. They were having far too good a time about this.

The hilarity didn't die down until Walsh arrived, and even he couldn't quite hide the grin on his face as he heard the song booming out across the field. Finally, though, he acted to restore some order and the boys settled down to get changed and help fetch out the gear.

As he organised the boys to complete their warm-up and set up a few light drills, Walsh watched the mist curling around the trunks of the trees along the edge of the field.

'So much for summer,' he muttered.

Chris was stretching out his hamstrings. He followed Walsh's stare.

'It's all right for you,' Walsh commented. 'You've got a week in America to look forward to.'

'In New Jersey, tourist centre of the world,' Chris reminded him.

'Yeah, but you get a day in New York and another in the mountains. Sounds better than a foggy, damp summer in Oldcester.'

The exchange trip was just a few weeks away. For the first time in a while, Chris felt a twinge of excitement about it.

'How's the arm?' asked Walsh.

'On the mend.'

'Don't do anything to aggravate it today, then,' Walsh instructed Chris. 'If you're not fit for Saturday, Sean will have my hide.'

'I've taken some pain-killers; I'll be fine.'

That seemed to satisfy Walsh, who didn't pay Chris any special attention after that. He rounded up the late arrivals and hustled everyone into getting ready for the practice session.

Before they started, however, he had a few announce-ments to make about the forthcoming visit twelve of the squad would be making to America. There was a lot of excitement among the lucky dozen, Chris included. They were looking forward to getting to grips with their opposite numbers from Mount Graham High School once again. For about the thousandth time, stories were told of particular incidents from the first leg of the exchange, when Mount Graham had come to Oldcester.

'They really improved over one week of training with United,' said Polly. 'We were lucky to beat them in that mini-tournament.'

This wasn't a view shared by all of the squad. Some of the others were certain that when the Colts went out to New Jersey, they'd thrash every team they were put up against.

It took Walsh a long time to quiet the chatter. He'd never got the hang of saving these announcements until after practice . . .

Just to make things worse, he then chose to talk about the trials at the weekend. As well as Chris, Rory, Russell Jones, Zak and Stamp were all invited.

'After the way they played against us last time, I bet United are going to have a big clear out of the youth team,' Tollie observed. 'You guys are bound to get in.' He looked quite jealous. No-one offered him any sympathy – Tollie wasn't one of the best players the Colts had; left back had been a bit of a problem position for them over the last few years.

The Colts senior squad, with the boys who were older than Chris and his team, were also going to supply a few candidates for the trial. Everyone had high hopes that several of them would make it into the new school. However, it meant that by this time next week the Colts could be stripped of some of their best players. Walsh's job was to start rebuilding, and to make sure that those who stayed in the team continued to improve. There was always another year.

'OK,' he announced, clapping his hands. 'Finish your warm-ups, then we'll go once round the field.'

'That'll make a change,' remarked Tollie.

'Oh, well, if it's a change you're after, we'll run a little further!' snapped Walsh, pointing out the new route with his finger. 'Down to the gate, behind the wood, back up the river path, then round the pitch.' He had turned full circle as he showed them what he wanted them to do; as he came back to the front, he had his whistle between his lips. He gave one sharp blast. 'Off you go!'

A light jog wasn't going to hurt, Chris decided, so he set off with the pack towards the gate. The guys at the front were whooping with amusement as they kicked through the soft wisps of mist hanging over the grass. Chris knew he was fast and strong enough to catch any of them, but he didn't want to jar his arm, so he took it slowly, at about the same pace as Mac and Rory Blackstone.

Even that felt a little uncomfortable, so he waved them on. Maybe he was trying too much too soon. He considered turning back along the main drive, but decided that he ought to stretch his legs out a bit and complete the run, even at a reduced pace.

A few of the leaders were cutting the corner now, angling away from the drive towards the little patch of woodland that separated the edge of the campus from the river. There was a trail – of sorts – through the chestnut and beech trees, winding along close to the wall until it emerged on to the path that led from the sports field to the river gate, from where there was access on to the towpath.

The air had taken on a strange, echoing quality. The shouts of the leaders – Zak's stern words of encouragement among them – were being muffled by the mist, which seemed a little deeper over by the trees. The cooler air, closer to the river and under the trees, was allowing the summer fog to condense more quickly.

Rory and Neil Tate, a new recruit, were the last two before Chris. He saw them disappear into the gloom of the small spinney about twenty metres ahead. He could still hear some of the others. Chris followed them into the shade of the trees.

He slowed his pace even more as he hit the trail, fearful that if he stumbled over a tree root, he might really do himself some damage. Under the canopy of the leaves, everything seemed quite peaceful. Chris picked his feet up, trying to make sure he got as much benefit from the run as he could.

A bird dashed across the trail ahead of him, so close to his face that he almost jumped back. He looked off the track into the bushes to see where it had gone, but the mist was really quite thick in there. The sun must have gone in too, he decided. It was becoming quite dark and spooky . . .

Chris felt the hairs on the back of his neck stand up. The last time he had felt like this had been in Memorial Park, just before the first time he'd met William. Chris slowed to a standstill. Was Billy Murdoch going to make an appearance once again?

Chris stood quite still in the dark heart of the wood. Nothing happened. The silence was absolute, save for the hammering of Chris's own heart. He was completely alone.

He waited for quite a while before he realised that this was foolishness and set off again. After all, even he didn't believe that William was a ghost any more, did he? And even if he did, what connection could William have had with this place, so far from the city centre? Back in 1914, Spirebrook had been separated from Oldcester proper by a wide belt of countryside; this had all been open countryside, save for the chemical works further along the river, close to the back of where Spirebrook Comprehensive now lay. The university only dated back to the 1960s.

He set off along the winding trail once more, sensing some light ahead that was probably the edge of the spinney.

He wasn't disappointed that William hadn't appeared. In fact, he was quite glad. After four days of confusion, he was just starting to get himself back together. He needed to focus on the trials. That was the important goal, not some half-baked chase after a phantom.

As Chris took what he hoped was the last turn of the trail, he felt the surface under his feet change from hard earth to soft grass. Immediately, he stopped. He knew this place well enough to know that the trail led directly on to the tarmac path. Somehow, he'd managed to stray off the trail before he'd left the spinney. The mist was actually so thick here that he could barely see his hand in front of his face.

He backed up a few paces, finding the trail once more. He groped around, getting his geography sorted out by finding where the trees ended and the open park of the campus began. Each time he thought he had it, he stepped on to grass once more. He just couldn't find the path.

Logically, he knew the way to get out of this. The wall was off to his left somewhere. If he found that and turned right, he'd reach the gate and then he'd have the path under his feet once again.

Edging around trees and low bushes, Chris felt his way around the edge of the woodland. After about ten metres, the trees fell away from his right-hand side. The feeling of being in a wide open space made him panic for a moment, but then he felt hard soil under his feet again. Some kind of wide path. Allowing for the fact that he couldn't see anything, he decided to follow it. At least he was bound to reach somewhere he recognised.

Stepping forward slowly, like a blind man robbed even of the slightest sound to guide him, Chris shambled forward a few more steps, then stopped. Had he just heard something? A gentle lapping sound? Like water?

He took another step and then, for a split second, he was falling.

The hand that grabbed him was solid enough, and there was no mistaking the strength of the arm that pulled him back. One moment the ground had fallen away from under Chris's feet, the next he was back on the path, his good arm safely fastened in William's grip.

'What are you doing?' the young man cried, his face full of alarm. 'You nearly fell into the river!'

'I can't have!' replied Chris, in a thin, astonished voice. 'I didn't come through the river gate!' He looked around desperately, trying to get a fix on where he was.

'Pearly gates, more like!' scoffed William. 'See here . . .' He led Chris a half-pace forward and stooped down. Copying him Chris could see the bank drop away sharply to the black surface of the river below.

'It's not possible . . .' Chris breathed.

'You weren't committing suicide, were you?' asked William. 'A young lad like you? You've got your whole life in front of you; what about this trial you've got coming up?'

Chris looked directly at William for the first time. '. . . wasn't committing suicide,' he told him. 'You can let go o—

my arm. I mean it, I'm not going to kill myself.'

'Glad to hear it,' said William. 'I knew a bloke what killed himself once. Messy business.'

They stepped back from the edge a little further. Chris looked around, trying to orientate himself.

'I can't see a thing,' he confessed.

'Aye, it gets really thick along here sometimes. Worst stretch of the river for sudden fogs is this. I used to come fishing just up from here. Miserable place, but the fishing was good.'

Chris couldn't believe they were having this conversation. William had just stepped out of the mist and plucked him from possible drowning. And they were talking about *fishing*?

'William, what are you doing here?'

The man looked genuinely surprised at the question. He scratched at the base of his neck. 'Well, you might say I was looking out for you. I know we didn't arrange to meet for another practice after last time, but I remembered you saying you practised on Wednesdays, so I came looking for you. It wasn't easy finding where you played! What a strange place to come!' He laughed briefly, then became serious. 'I wanted to say goodbye,' he told Chris.

'Goodbye?'

William wasn't looking at Chris. He was staring downstream, in the direction of Spirebrook and the bridges that crossed the river there.

'Aye. I've got to go away, you see. I'll not be around to help coach you any more.'

'Where are you going?' asked Chris. He had just realised that William, for the first time ever since Chris had first met him, wasn't wearing his old United shirt. He had a plain, collarless white shirt on and a heavy, ragged coat, belted at the waist. There was a battered old bag in his hand, tied with string.

'Overseas,' said William. 'I've . . . got to get away from here for a time.'

Chris instinctively knew why. 'Jack Schwarz,' he said.

Once again, William seemed caught off-balance. 'That's right! Do you know him too?'

'Yes,' said Chris. 'I've got to know him recently.'

William sucked in air through his teeth, as if he didn't trust himself to open his mouth straight away. 'I'll not speak ill of him behind his back,' he said at last. 'Let's just say we don't get on.'

Chris nodded. 'He's not half the player you are, William.' He had no idea why he said that, but the effect was immediate.

'Listen, I don't mean to let you down about the training and all,' William said. 'I just have to go. Do you understand?'

Chris nodded again.

'I want you to have something, though . . .' William bent down, put his ratty old case on the ground and started to unlace the string. The bag almost burst open when he'd untied the knot. He tucked a few odds and ends back inside, then brought out the item that had been at the top of the pile.

'It's a bit big on you,' he said. 'But you'll grow into it.'

The cotton was so new it almost crackled. The colours were vibrant – a rich, dark blue and a vivid, hot red. It laced at the neck and the collar was stiff with starch. On the breast there was an embroidered club badge.

'William, I . . .'

'You must take it, lad. I want you to wear it the first time you play for the club.'

'I'm not sure they'll be wearing shirts like this by the time I play,' said Chris. He still hadn't taken his eyes off it.

'What? Do you think football is like a fashion show? They don't change their shirts every few years like ladies' dresses, you know!'

Chris opened his mouth, but the reply died there. In the end, all he could say was, 'Thanks.'

William was tying up his case once more. He seemed in a hurry to get going. 'There's a train through in less than half an hour,' he said, with a nod in the direction of the bridges down-river from where they stood.

'Does this mean I'll never see you again?' asked Chris.

William shrugged. 'Who knows?' he said. He stood upright drawing in a deep breath. 'I hope I come back. All my life, I've wanted to play for Oldcester United. If I never did . . .' He paused, trying to find the right words to express how he felt

In the end he gave up. 'I'm not sure what I'd do. It'd be like I'd never really lived my life, you know?'

Chris knew exactly what he meant.

William clearly sensed what was going through Chris's mind. 'Oh, I'd not be worried, if I were you. You'll sail through these trials, and in a few more years, you'll be playing every Saturday in front of 40,000 folk who'll all know your name. You didn't need me to show you anything really; you just need to start believing in yourself.'

Chris wasn't sure that was true (and not just the idea of a 40,000 crowd at Star Park). If nothing else, that one session on the old railway depot had given Chris a skill he hadn't known before.

He didn't say anything about that, though. William was about to leave.

'I wish there was something I could do, to help you with your dream,' he said at last.

William smiled, and stuck out his hand. 'Goodbye, Chris,' he said. 'At least you'll not forget me, eh?'

'You can bet on that,' Chris assured him.

They were finished. William had to be going, and there was nothing left to say, except . . .

'William?'

'Aye?'

'How do I get back . . . from here?'

'Well, you could always walk along the river bank,' suggested William. Then he thought about what he'd advised. 'Still, perhaps not, eh? Look, just go that way, and you'll pick up a footpath across the meadow. Keep going, and there's the road into Oldcester not half a mile beyond.'

Chris looked off in the direction he was pointing. The mist was still so thick it hid everything from view. Chris had a moment when he feared he would be lost in it for ever, but he knew that once William departed, the fog would rise.

'Good luck,' he said.

William stuck out his hand, and they shook on it.

'I'll see you,' he said, and with that he turned away, striding along the river bank with the confidence of someone who could see the towpath as clear as day. Within seconds, the

139

mist had swallowed him up. Even his footsteps became muffled and then silenced.

Chris turned as well, following the direction William had suggested. He had already decided not to reveal anything of this latest encounter to the others. After all, he knew what they would say – that he had lost himself in the fog and passed through the gate without noticing. That William was following him. Some of them might even get worried at that last idea, fearing that William might be more dangerous than they had supposed before.

But Chris knew. And this time he even had evidence, though it was evidence he could never fully share with a soul. How could he expect anyone to believe a ghost had given him an 80-year-old football shirt in pristine condition?

Chris clutched it close to his breast, not sure if he believed it all himself. However, it was with a new confidence about the trial and everything that would come after, that Chris stepped into the future.

Seventeen

In some ways it was hard to tell how the day was different to any other. It was cold and damp, though the sun made a brave effort to break through some low cloud and warm the barren, muddy fields in which they were stationed. The trenches were still ankle-deep in water, and their quarters were dark, smelly and freezing cold.

William had never known what a good Christmas was, but even he knew this one was the very worst.

Some resourceful soul had found some holly, which he had pinned to the trench wall. Others had made cards from whatever paper or card they could find. There was talk of some special rations and a few hymns after dinner.

These small efforts to make something out of Christmas in the trenches almost made it worse. It was a reminder of what they were missing; home, family, friends. For William, it was the prospect of missing the Bank Holiday fixture. Oldcester always seemed to play well on Boxing Day. Some of the fans said it would make sense to feed them on chicken and Christmas pudding all year round. He'd never missed a game, not since he was old enough to walk to the ground and sneak in through a gap in the fence. The men had passed him down to the front of the stand, rolling him down above their heads like he was a sack of potatoes.

There was no football at home this year. And no prospect that they would be going home to welcome in the next season. When they had boarded the train for France, the officers had said they should be home by Christmas. Even in that first December, many of the men knew that the war would drag on for much longer than the generals told them.

William first realised something was up when he heard

movement in the trench outside. There were excited whispers and a lot of running feet.

Corporal Dooley put his head through the opening of their billet.

'Murdoch, get out here – you must see this!'

William went out into the trench, immediately becoming aware of the chill in the air. To his amazement, many of his mates were standing on the fire step, looking over the parapet of the trench. Normally, this would be suicide, since the German snipers were only about 80 yards away. However, there was no shooting – in fact, very few of the men in the trench even had their rifles to hand.

William found a space and climbed up to take a look out into no man's land. Everyone was looking off to the right, shouting and cheering. William couldn't believe his eyes. In the space between the barbed wire, on ground that was pitted with shell holes, two teams were playing football. One wore the drab khaki of the British army, the other wore German field grey.

The goals were makeshift and the ball looked as if it was soaked through and as heavy as lead, but it was football, here at the front line. Germany v. England.

'That's the mob from your home town, isn't it?' asked Dooley.

William nodded.

'They're taking a hammering. I've seen the Krauts score two goals just while I've been watching.'

William continued to stare at the distant game, wondering if he knew any of the players in khaki. Several of the Oldcester United team had signed up in the first few days of the war. He wondered if any of them had lived long enough to take part in this amazing game. There was no way of telling. Ever since William's unit had been posted right next door to his home town regiment, he had been sure he would bump into someone in knew. In fact, the two units never mixed, not even when they were moved back from the front line.

And there was one thing you soon got used to in the trenches – everyone looked the same. That suited William fine – if he was just another Tommy in a dirty uniform and a tin helmet, no-one would ever be able to confront him about that last day he'd spent in Oldcester. That was a day he was trying very hard to forget.

Dooley was looking across no man's land, ignoring the game.

'We should play that lot opposite,' he muttered. 'We'd hardly do any worse.'

Several of the others in the platoon muttered in agreement.

'We don't have a ball,' William pointed out.

'No, more's the pity,' sighed Dooley, looking quite sad for a moment. Suddenly, he perked up. 'Aye, aye — what's this?'

It appeared that someone on the other side had had the same idea, and the Germans had a ball with them. A white flag had been raised, and a tall man with close-cropped blond hair was leaning out from the German trenches, waving a leather ball. 'Hey, Tommy!' he called. 'Fussball!!!'

'It's a challenge!' gasped Dooley. 'Cheeky blighters. I'll give them bloomin' foos-ball.'

He stripped off his tunic, and stepped up on to the trench parapet.

'Aye, Fritz! We'll play! Only it's called football — and the British invented it, all right?'

There was a lot of jeering from the other side.

'Come on, George,' Dooley was urging. 'And you, Chalkie. Honour's at stake. We'll be playing for our country! Hugh, are you in?'

Dooley selected the rest of the side, captain by self-appointment. A couple of the lads didn't want to play — they were sure they'd be in trouble. As Dooley hunted around for the last few names, William stripped off his tunic.

'I'll play, Corp,' he said, stepping up.

'Good for you, Murdoch! Is that eleven of us, then? Taffy, you go in goal. What about you, Billy, where shall you play?'

'Full back,' William said firmly.

'Good show! Right, come on you lot, let's show these Jerries what a real game of football is like, eh?'

William followed the others through the wire and out into no man's land. An equal number of equally nervous-looking Germans were coming the other way. There was a huge cheer from the trenches on both sides. William could feel his heart beating faster and his stomach churning.

A half mile away, the Old Pals were going down in heavy defeat, unable to stop the Germans from scoring almost at will.

'They'll not get past me, though,' thought William, watching as Dooley shook hands with his opposite number and a rough pitch was marked out. 'I'll not lose the first real game I've ever played . . .'

They marked out the goals with tunics and greatcoats, and managed – through a mixture of broken English and sign language – to organise the coin toss and which team would play from which end. A watch was found, and the owner pressed into service as referee. He borrowed a whistle from an officer.

A sharp blast on a whistle had long since come to have a different meaning for the men in the trenches. It usually signalled an attack, bayonets fixed, running through the mud and the wire while the other side poured machine gun fire into their ranks. When the whistle blew to start the game, some men flinched.

But today, it marked the beginning of something more important than war. This was football.

The business on the river bank could have been the end of the story, but for two things. The first of these was that Chris was determined that others should remember William Murdoch as clearly as he did. By donating the shirt William had given him to the club's museum, along with the book, plus anything else they could find out, Chris hoped that some kind of permanent memorial could be made to honour William's name.

The second thing wasn't so predictable. Although, seeing as it had to do with Nicky, maybe it was.

Before he could part with the book, Chris wanted to complete reading it. He shut himself away on the Thursday, turning down a chance to go to the cinema with the Fiorentini family in order to read the rest of the book and to copy as much as he could on to the computer.

It was pretty heavy-going. After leaving Oldcester, William had travelled to Derby, where he had joined the army. Training had been brutal, but he had come through it OK, and gone off to Flanders in the last few weeks of 1914. He had lied about his age in order to enlist, and no-one had ever asked him why he had chosen to join a different regiment than the Oldcester Old Pals.

The fighting had settled into the static, trench warfare that was to make this first global conflict so terrible. William had been appalled at what he saw. The officers were stupid, the conditions bleak. Long periods of boredom were broken up only by sudden attacks and counter-attacks, with hundreds of men on both sides sacrificed to take a few yards of ground. It was senseless slaughter.

William had survived his first battle in November when many of the lads he had trained with were mown down. It frightened Chris just how often William would record the name of a friend on one page, only to say he was dead on the next.

The only cheering part of the whole account was when William talked about the game of football he had played with the other lads of his unit against the Germans from the trenches opposite. It was a single day of humanity in what would turn out to be four years of war.

Chris finally finished reading and recording the fragile book late that night. That evening, he made an appointment to see Mr Swain the following day, to see if there was anything he could tell Chris about William Murdoch. Although the man himself was at work, his wife said she was sure he'd be glad to help out. Following that, he rang Star Park and asked if he could see Dennis Lively about something important. Unfortunately, the chairman wasn't in and wouldn't be back until late on Friday. His secretary said he was planning to attend the trial on Saturday – perhaps Chris could see him then?

That would have to do. In fact, it would be a nice way to celebrate getting through the trial. Whether or not he made it through the selection process, Chris was determined to make the day one to remember.

'I thought all this William stuff was finished,' moaned Nicky over the phone.

'It is really,' Chris replied. 'I just want to see if Swain has anything.'

There was silence at the other end. Clearly Nicky was trying to decide if he was prepared to waste any more of his time on Operation William.

'What time are you seeing Smith?'

'Swain,' Chris corrected immediately, then he added: 'Two o'clock.' It was eleven o'clock Friday morning, just 24 hours before the trials started. 'Why, do you have something in mind?'

'I just thought we could do something different,' said Nicky. 'Take our minds off Saturday a bit.'

'Why, Nicky – are you starting to get nervous?' Chris laughed.

'It's not for me,' Nicky insisted angrily. 'You're the one who needs something to distract you.' The louder he protested, the more Chris knew that the pressure was finally getting to his team mate.

'No, not any more. I'm raring to go,' said Chris. He let Nicky sweat for a moment, then relented. 'Still, I suppose we could do something. You want to meet up afterwards? We could catch a film, maybe. I'll meet you in town –'

'Nah!' said Nicky quickly. 'I'll come and find you. I'm not sitting around waiting for you to show up. You'll probably get kidnapped by aliens or something.'

Chris laughed, and he was still chuckling when he put the phone down a few minutes later. He felt good; he felt relaxed. From the moment he had stumbled out of the mist at the university on Wednesday, all the tensions of the week before had disappeared. The rest of the Colts were just about getting ready to organise a search party as he appeared. The group had come to the conclusion that Chris had managed to get confused in the gloom and had wandered off the path. They would even have found a way of explaining the shirt, had he shown it to anyone. As they had all said before, it could just be a replica, or a handmade copy made by David Kirke's mum. The book had been even more real, and no-one had believed in that. Chris had hidden the shirt under his own kit as he wandered back along the path, then quickly transferred it to his bag.

Everyone had a good laugh about the fog, making jokes about the *X Files* and how Chris was getting as weird to be around as Fox Mulder. Chris was happy for them to think what they liked. He didn't tell anyone about meeting William, or about how he had managed to get on to the towpath as if the wall wasn't there. There would be some explanation – perhaps Russell would insist that Chris had wandered through the gate without noticing.

He didn't really mind that he would never be able to convince the others that William was real (well, as real as ghosts could get, anyway . . .). He knew. He was sure. Kind of.

It didn't even matter that much any more whether Chris believed in William the ghost. William the person, the young man who had come so close to being able to play for Oldcester all those years ago, he was real.

Even if the guy Chris had encountered during the last week was nothing more than a poor, lonely misfit, taking on another man's identity like a new set of clothes, Chris had made William/Kirke a promise. He was going to make sure that the name of William Murdoch never vanished from view again.

Chris made another promise that Friday, this one to himself. His arm was still stiff, but it didn't hurt any more and he was hungry to play. He was ready for the trial.

He packed a few items in his school bag; a notepad and some pens, a mini tape recorder his father had bought for work a few years back and William's book. Finally, he took the shirt William had given him from the drawer he had hidden it in after he got back from Wednesday training.

'I'm going to wear this the first time I play for United,' he said. He'd have to persuade the club somehow, but that problem was a few years away yet.

He'd considered wearing it for the trials, but decided against it. It was supposed to be worn only by a first team player. That was what Chris would have to become. For the first time in weeks, he was sure that this was what lay in the future for him.

Why else would William have picked him out?

With the shirt folded on top of all the other gear, Chris set off for his meeting with Mr Swain. He was keeping his fingers crossed that the amateur historian would have something about William Murdoch in his records — one final piece of evidence to complete the collection.

As it turned out, Frank Swain knew Billy Murdoch better than just anyone alive. Chris was going to get closer to the truth than he really wanted.

Eighteen

Chris found Swain's place easily enough. It was just across Easter Road from the ground, along a quiet street of semi-detached houses, lined with newish cars. Swain's home wasn't quite in Star Park's shadow, as William's house in Warwick Street had been, but it was close enough.

No wonder Frank Swain was such a fan. Chris wondered idly what houses round this way cost. Maybe he could persuade his father that they should move . . .

As he worked out which was the right house, Chris saw there was a young lad of about his own age in the drive, knocking a match ball against the wall between the garage and the front door. He was two-footed, well balanced and quick. He played pass after pass against the brickwork, hitting the ball back again first time on the majority of occasions.

As he got closer, Chris realised that he recognised him. He was one of the lads already on the youth team books at Oldcester! Chris knew him from the trials the year before and the mini-tournament they had both been part of at the end of the Americans' exchange visit. The lad was a striker, like Chris. They hadn't been introduced, but Chris knew his first name. Alan. Alan Swain.

Small world.

'Alan, hi!' Chris announced himself as he stepped on to the drive.

The other lad turned quickly, startled. His face was sharp with annoyance at the interruption, and the worst of the unpleasantness didn't fade as he realised who he was seeing, even though a small smile crept across his lips.

'Hello,' he said. 'You come to see my dad?'

'That's right,' said Chris.

'He's running a bit late, some meeting at work. He should be back soon, though.'

'That's OK,' said Chris, still recovering from the shock of meeting someone he recognised. 'I'll wait, if that's OK.'

The boy shrugged, which seemed to mean yes. Chris took a longer look at him, refreshing his memory. Alan was perhaps two inches shorter than Chris, but he was a bit more solid. His hair was shaved close, so that he looked like a younger version of Forest's Steve Stone. He was wearing an ordinary T-shirt and track suit leggings, plus expensive trainers. The ball was badly scuffed from being used on the hard, gritty drive.

'Small world, eh?' Chris ventured, trying to fill the awkward silence. 'I had no idea you lived here. I didn't get your last name before. By the way, I'm Chri–'

'Chris Stephens, I know,' said Alan flatly. 'You're going to be at the trials on Saturday, I hear.'

'That's right,' said Chris carefully. There was something in Alan's tone that he wasn't sure of. The other boy was rolling the ball back and forth under his right foot, fists aggressively held on his hips.

'I know all about you. I've seen you play a few times, and not just at the mini-tournament, either.'

'Really?'

Alan's grin grew wider. 'I saw you play for the Colts a couple of times in the season. And one of the school games for Spirebrook.' Chris was amazed. Why had Alan done that? The other boy supplied the answer right away. 'Know your enemy, that's what my father always says.'

'I'm sorry?' gasped Chris, flustered.

'Don't you get it?' asked Alan. 'It's my place you're after. I play up front for the United youth team. Come Saturday, it's either me or you.'

Chris was tempted to make some excuse and go back another time, but he didn't want to back down in front of Alan Swain. Chris had never been faced with competition for a place in a team like this before. The Colts kept a small squad, and at school the team was always changing, giving different guys a

149

chance. But the United youth squad was a fixed number of players at each age. For each player who got in, another was left out. For those in the set-up already, Saturday's trial was going to be even tougher than it was for the new boys.

'It might not come to that,' he said. 'We could both make the side.'

The boy uttered a sharp barking noise that might have been a laugh, though it was well disguised. 'They'll not want us both. Too similar. No, it's either you or me, according to some of the coaches I've spoken to. You're meant to be Sean's favourite.'

Alan was giving Chris a long, hard stare, as if he was evaluating his opponent. It owed more to boxing than football.

'Want to knock around for a bit, until me dad comes home?' asked Alan, suddenly.

Chris wasn't sure about that idea at all! He held up his hands and stepped back a pace.

'I don't know . . . I've no kit . . .' he began.

'You've got your trainers, haven't you? That's all I've got. Come on, we'll take a few penalties against each other. Use the garage as a goal.'

Chris didn't want to get into some macho challenge before the trial. What would it prove? Besides, it would be just his luck to go in goal and put his arm out again. He thought about mentioning the injury to Alan, but decided it didn't make sense to point out a weakness to a potential rival.

At the same time, Alan's expression had changed, and Chris found himself wondering if Alan was more nervous about the weekend than he'd realised. He almost seemed to be pleading with Chris. 'Go on, you can shoot first,' he said.

He tossed the ball to Chris, who took it on his chest and caught it under his foot. Alan was already walking towards the garage door.

'In for a penny . . .' muttered Chris, and he put his bag to one side, near the front door. He took the ball back to the entrance to the drive, about eight or nine metres away from the garage. There was a slight slope upward, which meant he couldn't steady the ball properly. He had to roll it forward a fraction from under his trainer, set himself and strike before the ball rolled back.

He hit the first shot with very little pace on it, straight at

Alan's midriff. The boy caught the ball and rolled it back, grinning.

'You can do better than that!' he laughed.

Chris fired another shot, better aimed this time, high and to Alan's left. His practice partner spun quickly and managed to get a hand behind the shot, knocking it down on to the drive again.

'Can't you hit it any harder?' asked Alan. There was no mockery in his tone. Chris realised he was actually enjoying this.

'I'm worried about the windows,' Chris confessed.

'You're not going to hit them, are you?' laughed Alan, gesturing with his arm to show that Chris would have to go pretty wide to hit any glass. Chris had to admit that, even though the garage door wasn't a big target, he couldn't fail to hit it from less than ten metres.

He hit the next one with a bit more bite, low so that it skipped off the slope. Alan sprawled on one knee, got half a hand on it, but the ball still cracked against the metal door with a resounding, booming wham. He didn't even get that close to the next two, which both rebounded to Chris's feet without Alan getting a touch. Chris popped another one off with his left foot, which hit the inside of the 'post'. The one after that, he cut across with the outside of his left foot. Even at pace and over a short distance, the ball swerved a little. Alan clapped his hands.

'I can only do that off my right foot,' he confessed.

'I only really learned to do it over the last year,' Chris said in reply, starting to warm to Alan Swain a little. 'Even now, the outswinger moves a lot better than the one that comes back in.'

Alan nodded, and trotted off to fetch the ball from the lawn where it had ended up after the last shot. 'I saw you get a goal with a swerving shot a few weeks back,' he said.

'I'm still amazed you went to all that trouble,' Chris replied.

Alan laughed, a little bit more genuinely this time. 'It's my dad's idea. He says the more you know about who you're playing against, the better your chances against them. We normally try to see all the other teams I'm going to be playing against, and when the coaches started talking about how you were going to be coming up for my place in the squad again, we found out where you played and came to take a look.'

Chris was completely amazed. If parental dedication counted for anything, Alan's place at United was as safe as houses.

'He's just bonkers about football,' said Alan. 'Lives and breathes it. He was never quite good enough to play League football, and it always got to him. Grandad used to play for United, ages ago. He wanted my dad to follow him into the team, but he just couldn't make it.'

Chris nodded to show that he understood. He'd seen the sort before, frustrated, not-quite-good-enough players who had tried to push their sons to be that little bit better. They stood on the touchlines at school games, swearing at the linesmen and yelling stupid advice. Chris always felt sorry for guys with fathers like that; his own dad was really pleased that Chris was doing well, but he never interfered with what the coaches were teaching Chris, and was always there just to support, never to criticise.

'That can't be easy,' he said.

Alan smiled. 'You've no idea . . .' he sighed, but it was clear that he wasn't too damaged from having a fanatic for a father. Alan was all right.

'You say your grandad used to play for United?' Chris asked, aware that he was becoming a bit of an expert on the names and faces of long-ago United players. 'When was that?' He was trying to remember if he'd seen the name Swain on any of the lists he had been going through.

Was that a warning tingle in the back of his mind, he wondered in the same moment. What's that doing there?

'Ages ago. He was really old, my grandad. Like, over a hundred. He had a telegram from the queen and everything. He only died last year.'

'I'm sorry,' said Chris. His brain was trying to do the maths. One hundred years old, so Alan's grandad was born at the end of the nineteenth century. He'd be twenty just before 1920, say. That probably meant he'd played just after World War One. Chris had looked at lists of players from that decade, trying to find if any of the players who had been in the team before the war survived to play afterwards. 'What was his

152

name?' Chris asked. 'I thought I knew all the Oldcester players from back then, but I don't remember anyone called Swain.'

'Oh, the family name wasn't Swain back then; it got changed.'

The warning bell was clanging even louder now, as if it was saying, 'Now do you see it?' Chris's conscious mind hadn't picked up on all the signs, though. That only started to see the danger after he asked, 'So what was his name, then?'

'Schwarz,' said Alan, smiling. 'Jack Schwarz.'

That name knocked Chris almost off his feet. Alan was looking at him quizzically, so Chris knew his shock must be written all over his face.

The best response he could manage was to repeat the name back at Alan. 'Jack Schwarz?'

'Yes,' said Alan, with a little nervous laugh in his voice. 'Why, do you know the name?'

'I've – uh! – read it somewhere . . .' muttered Chris, lamely.

Alan was quite pleased with this. 'Really? Cool! He played when he was just sixteen, but then the war broke out. He joined up in 1914, on the first day of the war! He had to change his name, you see, because Schwarz sounds German. So he picked Swain. And he saw the war through to the end. Can you imagine?'

At that moment, Chris was barely capable of breathing, never mind imagining anything.

'And . . . he – uh! – played? After the war?'

'Yes,' Alan replied proudly. 'He was quite a star back then, or so he told me. My dad says there are photos and stuff, but I've never seen them.'

'Oh,' Chris answered, while his mind tried to grope for something more meaningful.

'Then later on, he became a policeman, but he got slung out for being a bit heavy-handed. He only started a family during the Second World War. He never really liked kids, you see. He said they were always causing trouble. Back when he was a kid, they'd come round, nicking stuff from his father's market stall and –'

'Have you always lived round here?' Chris asked quickly. This was all getting a bit close to home.

'Yeah,' said Alan. 'My dad bought this place just after Star Park was opened. The new one, that is. He said him and grandad had always lived really close to the very first Star Park, and that he would never get used to having to walk a long way to see United play. They were a lot alike, him and grandad.'

The warning bell was still rattling away in Chris's mind.

'Yeah? How?' he asked. Somehow, he wasn't at all sure he was going to like the answer.

'My dad never liked kids much either. Still doesn't, I guess.' He laughed. Chris felt sorrier for Alan than before. 'And he started a family really late, when he was nearly forty, just like grandad. It's weird having a grandad who was born in the last century. He'd talk about stuff that you normally just read in history books, only he was there himself.'

Chris smiled weakly. Every instinct he had was yelling at him to get away from there, but he couldn't figure out why. The Schwarz family had always had it in for William, not him. Neither Alan nor his father could know that Chris had discovered William's notebook and that he had already read the truth about what had happened back then. He was just a rival striker; it wasn't like they could bear him any grudge.

There was another reason why Chris couldn't leave. He knew that Alan's father and grandfather had lied about the Swain connection with United. Jack Schwarz/Swain had already been rejected by the club before the war started, and William's book said that Jack was still in Oldcester in September – he couldn't have joined up on the first day of the war. As for him being a star after the war, Chris doubted it. Would Grandpa Swain have even got into the side if better players hadn't had their lives wasted on the battlefield?

Chris wasn't sure if he was going to set the record straight for the Swains, but he wasn't going to let them claim credit for something that should have belonged to William. Alan had mentioned pictures. Was it possible that William was in any of them?

I'm staying, Chris told himself silently. Turn off the alarm bells. All I have to do is keep quiet about why I'm interested . . .

'What does your dad do?' he asked Alan.

'He's an ex-copper too,' Alan sighed. 'Just like grandad

again. He retired a few years ago, and works part-time as a security guard so that he can spend more time helping me with football. I shouldn't say this, but for some things it would be better if – oh, oh, here he comes.'

The alarm bells were ringing even louder as Chris turned round to get his first look at Frank; kid-hating ex-copper, kid-hating security guard and son of the infamous Jack Schwarz/Swain. As soon as he saw him, Chris knew that he was even worse than any other fanatical touchline father he'd ever seen. Frank Swain was worse than just a fanatic, he was a complete nutter.

It wasn't that Chris had suddenly become a better judge of people, able to spot the really strange ones at a glance. He knew Frank Swain. And, what was worse, Frank Swain knew him.

'Well, well,' the man sneered through his yellowing, spiky teeth. 'Look what the cat's dragged in.'

It shouldn't have been possible, but there it was.

Frank Swain was the same security guard who had chased after Chris and Nicky when they'd peeked over the wall of the Technology Park. He was even wearing his uniform. Chris found himself staring at the ugly mouth, with the stained railings instead of teeth. He didn't dare look away.

'Do you know who this is?' asked Alan.

'Of course I do!' snarled his father. 'This is Chris Stephens, the kid who's after your place in the team!'

'I know . . .' Alan started.

'He's also a little troublemaker who sticks his nose in where it doesn't belong and gets people fired from their job!'

Neither Alan nor Chris understood that remark. Chris was wondering if there was any way he could dodge past Mr Swain in the narrow driveway. He'd be more than happy to have this chat another day.

'What's happened?' asked Alan.

'I've been fired!' Swain roared. 'Some woman complained to the company about me, and I've been given my cards.' He jabbed a finger in Chris's direction. 'I reckon it was that nosy cow who rescued you in Easter Road! That makes sense. She looks the type to cause trouble!'

'Rescued?' cried Alan, completely in the dark. 'What is all this about?'

Chris didn't think it wise to try and enlighten him about what had happened earlier in the week. 'You knew who I was, even then . . .' he whispered, as much to himself as to Swain.

'Of course! That's why I came after you, and not your greasy little mate. I was going to haul you off in front of Mr Lively, or your mate Sean Priest, until that sticky-beaked lawyer cow got involved.'

'People know that I'm here,' Chris said suddenly, frightened at the ugly tone in the man's voice.

Swain laughed. 'What? You think I'm going to hurt you or something? I'm not that stupid! I'll find another way to deal with you, another day.'

Chris was still frozen to the spot. He forced himself to edge slightly to one side. 'I'd better be going,' he began.

'What's your hurry?' snarled Swain, still blocking the way. He was trying to sound harmless and innocent, which only made things worse. Chris remembered his bag and its precious contents. He looked back towards the front door, then cursed himself for making it so obvious. Swain had seen the gesture and quickly headed for the porch, sweeping up Chris's bag and opening the front door in one quick movement.

'I thought you had some questions you wanted to ask me,' he said, grinning.

Chris wondered if he could abandon the bag, but he knew he would never see the precious contents again if he did. Swain had opened up the door and was going inside. Chris looked at Alan, whose eyes were wide with shock.

'I don't understand . . .' he began.

'It'll be OK,' said Chris, wondering if he was trying to convince Alan or himself. 'Your dad and I had a bit of an argument, that's all. I'll just come and get my bag back, and then I'll leave. I don't want any trouble.'

Alan led the way inside. The hall was narrow and dark. Alan found his father in the front room, sitting in his favourite armchair. The bag was on the floor at his side.

'Come in, boys, come in!' Swain called, in mock welcome. 'Put the kettle on, Alan, there's a good lad. And fetch a drink for our guest.'

Chris stepped into the room. Just as he imagined, it was a shrine to Oldcester United and its history. There were pictures on every square centimetre of wall, and framed photographs and books on every shelf. A round table in the bay window was groaning under vast piles of programmes, notebooks and more books. Under the table, and at various other points around the room, there were cardboard boxes with more photographs, magazines and newspaper clippings.

'This isn't the half of it!' Swain boasted. 'The back room is stacked even higher! If there's anything you want to know about Oldcester United, I'm your man.'

It occurred to Chris that the question he most wanted to ask was, How do I get out of here?, but he kept that one to himself. Perhaps Swain wasn't such an expert in that area – or maybe he was. Either way, Chris didn't want to confront the issue just yet.

For now, fighting to keep calm, Chris decided to play along with the pretence that he wasn't frightened, and that his being in this house was a pure matter of choice.

'I need my notebook,' he said. Swain gestured at the bag, but he didn't move it any closer. Chris crossed the room cautiously, trying to find an angle from which he could get into the bag without getting too close to Swain. As he reached for it, Swain fixed his fingers around one of the handles. The idea of snatching the bag hadn't occurred to Chris before then. Just as well.

Knowing that the shirt was at the top of the bag, and the book inside it, Chris tried to avoid opening the bag too widely as he groped inside for his notebook and pen. All the time, he kept his eyes on Swain. The man was looking back at him, his eyes fierce and bright with menace.

Still searching for a pen, Chris's fingers closed around the mini recorder. Without thinking, he pressed the record button, then quickly found the items he was supposed to be looking for. He pulled them out and stepped back.

There was nowhere to sit except the floor. Chris found some space and squatted on the threadbare carpet. At the same time, Alan came back, nervously handing him a can of 7-Up.

'So, what is it you're looking for?'

Chris decided to stall for a minute. 'Are you really writing a book? A history of the club?'

'Yes,' said Swain, grinning and puffing out his chest. 'I've been working on it for years. All these pictures and stuff, they've been loaned to me by other fans, or people connected with the club. It's taken me this long just to catalogue them all, and there's more stuff coming in all the time.'

Which was as good as saying that he wasn't writing anything, just collecting all the stuff and hoarding it.

Chris opened the can and took a sip. His mouth was dry and the drink was ice cold. He perked up a little, opening the pad to write.

'OK, here's what I was looking for. I want to know if there are any photos or other stuff from before the First World War. I'm interested in any of the players who joined the services.'

That seemed vague enough to cover his real interest. Beside him, Alan added, 'I've told him about grandad.'

'Yes!' boomed Swain senior. 'There's a story straight off. The club signed him at the back end of the 1913/14 season. He was just sixteen. They put him straight into the first team. He played six games that year, and was going to play centre half the following season. But as soon as the war came along, he joined up and he was a hero, too. After the war he played five seasons, before he had to pack it in.'

Chris made a point of writing this all down, although he didn't believe that much of it. From what he'd read in William's book, Jack Schwarz had played a few reserve games, but Forbes, the team manager up to the war, had decided he didn't have what it took. So it could only have been after the war, when so many of the better players had been killed or maimed, that Schwarz had won a place under a different manager. Those had been indifferent years for United, too, as far as Chris could remember.

He had real doubts about the hero stuff, too.

'What about some of the others?' asked Chris. 'Some of the ones who didn't come back?'

He realised that he'd changed the subject just a little too quickly for Swain's liking. The man could probably have enjoyed bragging about his father's imaginary exploits for hours.

'What about them?' he snarled.

'Do you have any pictures, things like that? Everything the club had was lost in a fire, they say . . .'

Chris thought he saw a glint of delight in Swain's eye as he heard that. Was it possible that he knew something about the destruction of the old ground?

'It was a bad one, no mistake. That was when they left the old Star Park, the one over by the station, for good. The club bought land by the river and built a new stadium. That one lasted until the 1980s, when it was pulled down and the new one built.'

'So . . . did everything get destroyed?' Chris asked. Just outside his line of sight, he could feel Alan fidgeting nervously.

'Maybe,' said Swain, grinning. 'Maybe not.'

He wasn't going to make this easy. Chris wondered how to get the information he wanted.

'What about the local paper? Didn't they print team pictures back in those days?'

'They did,' replied Swain, rising to his feet suddenly. He crossed to one of the many boxes and pulled a scrapbook of cuttings from inside. He leafed over a few pages, then dropped the book on to the floor in front of Chris. It was open on a page that showed a yellowing square cut from a newspaper with a blurred image of the 1913/14 team on it. The names of the team members were clear enough, but the picture quality was so poor they could have been tailor's dummies for all the difference it made. It was just twenty indistinct faces with moustaches and short hair wearing identical striped shirts and baggy shorts.

'Printing back then wasn't always very clear,' Swain told him.

'What happened to the original?' asked Chris. He'd heard the paper was very good about keeping stuff like this.

'Given to the club,' Swain replied. Then he added, with a broad smirk, 'Lost in the fire.'

Chris was more convinced than ever that Swain knew what had happened. It made him angrier than he could control.

'The fire was in the mid-twenties, wasn't it? Was that about the time your father packed it in?'

'Could be . . .' said Swain, clearly enjoying the fact that Chris was slowly reaching towards the truth. Chris licked his lips and decided to try and pluck the words from between those vile yellow teeth.

'So, what really happened, Mr Swain? Did Jack get dropped? He was never really that good, after all . . .'

Swain didn't rise to the bait. 'Six seasons with the club, Stephens. He can't have been that bad.'

A good point, if it was true. Chris doubted it, and he doubted that Swain believed it to be true either. He knew how much both Jack and Frank hated children – perhaps it was also true that Frank knew the truth about his father and hated him for it.

'Yes, but how often did he play for the first team? I bet he spent most of the time in the reserves.'

'Nice try, son. But I've seen the facts. My father played for the first team, just like he told me and Alan he did.'

Of course. That was the family story, but if Frank had read all the stuff from back then, he'd know how much of that story was a lie.

Chris pushed a little harder. 'I don't know what happened in 1913/14 or after the war, Mr Swain, but if Jack told you he was going to play centre half for United in 1914/15, he was lying. Forbes had already dropped him from the squad. He didn't go straight off to war, either. He was in Oldcester in September that year at least, a month after the war started.'

At last, he had Swain rattled. He was sitting forward on the edge of the grubby plastic seat of his chair, his eyes narrow, his fists clenched. 'How do you know that?' he spat.

'Because I've read a kind of diary kept by the lad who took his place,' Chris replied, trying to keep his voice calm. 'I've seen Billy Murdoch's journal.'

That news hit Swain like a cold slap in the face. His skin went pale and his eyes clouded.

'Impossible!' he whispered.

'No, it's true,' said Chris.

The silence in the room was terrible. Chris fancied all he could hear was the air freezing. Swain's skin had changed from a florid pink, to pale white, and now to a chalky, greasy green-grey colour.

'Murdoch was nothing but a thief!' he gasped.

'That's not true,' Chris responded quickly. 'Your father hounded him from the first day he moved into Coventry Street, lied about him, bullied him and made his life a misery. All because Murdoch was a better player than your father could ever hope to be. In 1914, Forbes chose Billy rather than your father for the new season, but even then Jack didn't leave him alone. He managed to fake some evidence against Billy. My guess is that he got some of his mates to pretend they'd seen Billy stealing, or planted stuff at his house. When Jack told Forbes about it, Billy left Oldcester and joined the army. Billy Murdoch even went to war before your father did. And he was a real hero. He died in the front line, some time after Christmas.'

'You couldn't know all that . . .' spluttered Swain. 'Unless there really is a book.'

'It's true?' wailed Alan, at Chris's side. Chris could imagine how he was feeling, fed all this propaganda to make him behave and play like Frank Swain said Alan's grandfather had played. All a lie.

'How did you get to read this book?' demanded Swain, ignoring his son.

'I found it,' said Chris. 'Murdoch must have sent it home to his mother before he was killed. The last thing it says is that he expected to get some leave soon. Maybe he thought it would be one less thing to carry when he came home. He never made it.'

Swain was slowly recovering. Chris could see the spiteful side of his nature asserting control once again.

'Where is the book now?'

'Safe. Don't think I'd be stupid enough to have it with me.'

Immediately, Chris knew he was going to have to work on his lying. Swain leapt to his feet and dived into the bag. Later, Chris decided he'd have to be thankful that Swain didn't spot either the shirt or the tape recorder. But he found the book almost right away.

'Ha!' he cried triumphantly. He took a step towards Chris, kicking the bag towards him. Sitting on the floor made Chris appreciate just how much larger Swain was than him. A real giant. 'Get up.'

Chris rose slowly. Even standing he still felt completely

dominated by Swain's sheer size and ugly, brutal power.

'Of course you're that stupid,' he growled. 'Boys your age always are. You're every bit as dumb as my father said Murdoch was. Running off like that! And do you know how he died? Volunteering for a patrol, my dad said. What an idiot! Jack came home by keeping his head down. He got to play for United, even if it was only a dozen games. What did Billy Murdoch ever achieve?'

He reached out and grabbed Chris's injured arm. The grip was tight. Chris winced, but he couldn't hope to pull away.

Swain waved the precious book in Chris's face. 'And now this! Even after all these years, Murdoch's still trying to cause trouble, and he's still failing! You'll not ruin my father's reputation with this, Stephens.'

'What are you going to do?'

'I'll burn it, of course. We have a habit of burning things we don't like in this family.' He was grinning evilly now, sure that he had won. 'Pick up your bag!' he snapped.

Chris bent and fixed his left hand around the bag's handles. He was desperate to find a way to rescue the book, but how could he? And if he stayed, Swain might discover the shirt and the tape. Surely he had to just run for it?

'One last thing,' snarled Swain, and as he said it he let go of Chris's sleeve. Snapping his arm back, he whacked his closed fist against Chris's elbow.

The pain was so bad Chris thought he was going to faint. He swayed on his feet until Swain caught hold of him and pulled him upright, dragging him towards the door.

'You'll get more of that on Saturday,' he promised. 'You're not going to get through the trial – United needs a Swain in the side, not the likes of you!'

With those words ringing in his ears, Chris found himself tossed out on to the street. His arm was throbbing like crazy.

He picked himself up and staggered away from Swain's house. Was that laughter he could hear from inside? Chris couldn't be sure, but he knew one thing. After 80 years, he had just buried William Murdoch once and for all.

Nineteen

Oldcester United's London Road training ground was about four miles from Star Park, on the same side of the river but further from the city centre. A long, straight, tree-lined highway followed the course of an ancient Roman road through suburbs and past out-of-town shopping centres. At the end of it, on a corner, the training ground was surrounded by a smart green fence and tall, broad-leafed trees, stirring in the wind.

The sun was bright and warm. The afternoon threatened to be the hottest of the year so far. Traffic hissed along the road through the last puddles left by some overnight rain. Most of the cars were heading for the big supermarkets and the shopping mall at Palace Marina, but a steady stream was turning through the wide gates and into the less-than-spacious parking area behind the clubhouse.

At a little before 10.20am on that glorious Saturday, Chris stepped from his father's car. He went round to the boot to get his kit bag while his father waited to turn the key in the driver's door. When Chris was ready, they walked down to the edge of the training pitch to take a look at the bright stretch of green grass, freshly watered by the rain. Various exercises had already been laid out, traffic cones marking dribbling lanes or fenced-off areas for passing drills and skill tests.

On the far side, there was a separate fenced-off area with three side-by-side all-weather pitches. They wandered over there as well, watching the United training staff get ready for the day's activities, seeing who else was there, who had come to take part and who to watch.

Not a word was spoken before Mr Stephens looked to his watch and announced, 'It's just gone half-past.'

They turned back together and went back to the changing rooms and the small office where Sean Priest and the other training staff would be huddled between sessions. It was time to face up to the facts.

❀

Dr Loenikov hadn't been impressed.

'This really shouldn't be causing you any more pain, Chris,' he said. 'I was sure it wasn't that serious.'

'It's had a couple of knocks since I saw you last,' Chris said quietly, holding his right arm steady while Dr Loenikov pushed and prodded and probed. He winced as the doctor's fingers touched a particularly sensitive area around the bone of the elbow. It had been like that since the incident with Swain yesterday, the worst the arm had felt since the original injury.

'I can give you a pain-killing injection to get through today,' the doctor said, but his voice sounded doubtful. Chris and his father had already reached the same conclusion.

'If I play, and can't feel anything, couldn't I do some real damage?' Chris asked. Dr Loenikov gently released his arm and stepped back, thinking about what he had seen and felt.

'I'm afraid that's true,' he said. 'Really, you should go to the hospital and get an X-ray. It could be that the original injury is worse than I thought, or that this accident you had damaged the bone . . .' Chris was just starting to fear the worst when the doctor rocked back with a broad smile on his face. 'Or it could just be sore as a reminder to you that when your doctor says rest the arm, he doesn't mean you should go out playing ice hockey!'

'So, what do you think?' asked Mr Stephens, who was standing by the door, looking very thoughtful. 'Should he play?'

Dr Loenikov was delving inside a large cupboard in the corner of his surgery. He returned with a long blue sleeve of what looked like solid rubber, although Chris discovered it was surprisingly flexible. The doctor slid it up over Chris's hand and forearm, and then started to coax it gently and carefully over his elbow until it completely surrounded the joint. It gripped tightly, but Chris could just about manage to bend his arm, not that he really wanted to much.

164

'That should keep some of the knocks at bay,' the doctor said. 'That aside, I think Chris should have the injection and play. We all know how much today means, am I right?'

The two members of the Stephens family nodded in unison. Chris took a moment to decide what he wanted.

'Once again, doctor, we're really grateful,' said Mr Stephens. 'That's twice in a week we've taken advantage of you living so close.'

'Pah!' cried Dr Loenikov dismissively. 'It's nothing. If not for you, I would have to go shopping for garden furniture with my wife.'

They laughed. 'If there's anything I can do,' said Mr Stephens.

The Ukrainian's face grew brighter. 'Well, yes, there is . . . This trial, is it open to the public?'

'No,' replied Mr Stephens, 'I'm afraid not.'

Dr Loenikov didn't look too disappointed. In fact, that seemed to be the answer he had been looking for. 'But you could maybe get a pass or something?'

Chris began to understand. Clearly, garden furniture came some way down the list in Dr Loenikov's scheme of things. 'I think I know someone I can call,' he said.

'Good!' The doctor grinned. 'I think with an injury like that, you should have your GP close at hand, just in case, eh?'

Chris and his father made ready to leave.

'Besides,' Dr Loenikov added at the door, 'a little support never hurt anyone.' He pointed at the elastic bandage and laughed. It must have been a doctor thing.

Whatever system the club used to determine who could go to these things hadn't stopped the Fiorentini clan stepping out in vast numbers. Nicky emerged from the centre of a scrum of his immediate family, grandma, uncles, cousins and several others who looked so much alike that they could have been clones.

'Have you been to the police?' Nicky demanded by way of greeting.

'Fine, Nicky, how are you?' Chris responded. After leaving Swain's house, Chris had met up with Nicky and told him everything (later, he'd even told his father the complete story, which was something of a first). They'd played back the tape on the bus while heading back to Spirebrook. Nicky insisted it was proof of arson, assault and theft.

Chris wasn't so sure. After talking it over with his father, they'd decided not to go to the police straight away. There were a few other options to try first.

'You can't let Swain get away with it!' Nicky insisted.

'We're not going to,' Chris replied. 'But if you listen to the tape, he doesn't actually admit to anything. It's all nudges and winks. Half the time, the voice is so muffled, you can't hear what he's saying.'

'But he threw you on to the floor – deliberately!'

'We'd never be able to prove that,' Chris reminded him. 'It's just my word against his.'

'I'll say I saw it!' Nicky offered. It would almost have been true. Nicky had been waiting for Chris at the corner of the street. As Chris had dragged himself out of the drive, Nicky had seen him right away.

'That's called perjury,' said Chris. Nicky's face showed that he didn't know what Chris meant – either what the word was or what the problem would be with telling a small lie if it dropped Swain in trouble. Chris had no doubt that the entire Fiorentini family would swear they were just passing by Swain's house if it meant having revenge on him. The Fiorentinis had always had a soft spot for Chris and a softer spot for underdogs generally.

'Is he here yet?' asked Nicky, looking round. Chris knew this meant his friend's family had also discussed the possibility of Uncle Fabian and one or two cousins walking Mr Swain behind a building for a 'chat'.

'Just don't get involved, Nicky,' Chris pleaded. He could tell from Nicky's expression that the words had gone right over his head.

Uncle Fabian was calling from the edge of the pack of black-haired supporters, pointing at his watch. Nicky was already changed, wearing his United track suit over the away strip's shorts and socks, and a plain blue shirt. The signal was intended for Chris.

'You'd better get ready,' said Nicky.

'I have to see Sean first,' said Chris, moving off. His father

166

went over to see the Fiorentinis as he walked towards the clubhouse. They had decided last night that Mr Stephens wouldn't interfere.

Chris looked around, seeing who else he could recognise. He saw Bennett, the hard defender from Blackmoor Comprehensive, with whom he had had a running feud for years (now hopefully resolved); warming up nearby was Robert James, another first-rate defender, who played in a team with boys two or three years older; behind him was Andy Williams, a red-hot utility player from Milton Keynes who had been playing for Masham, one of the Colts' rival teams.

Trials day was one of the busiest in Priest's year, and there was an awkward moment when one of the coaching staff Chris didn't know so well stopped him before he reached the office. Chris showed him the pass he had been given at the gate, but it made no difference. Then he saw Doris, the woman from the window at Star Park. He was just wondering how she would react to him yelling 'Hey, Doris!' across the room (and deciding that he would sooner eat sand) when she looked up and saw him.

'You again,' she muttered, heading over to investigate. 'I don't know why we don't just give you a set of keys to everywhere.'

'Hello!' Chris said, trying to smile warmly. 'I was just explaining that I have to give some stuff to Sean – uh – Mr Priest.' He lifted the bag as evidence.

Doris didn't even look at it, or Chris. She took a quizzical look at the coach blocking Chris's way, who shrugged as if to say that he had no idea what was going on. Her lip twisting upward as if she'd tasted something unpleasant, Doris told him, 'You might as well let this one through. If you say no, you can guarantee Sean will just walk out of that door and overrule you anyway. I get the impression we're going to be seeing a lot of this nuisance from now on.'

And with that she turned on her heel and went off on her way.

It wasn't exactly a ringing endorsement, but the coach decided to play safe and led Chris to a door. He knocked once and opened it, telling those inside that there was someone to see Sean.

Moments later, Priest appeared at the door, looking tense as if the last-minute preparations were causing him more hassle than usual. He was talking over his shoulder to someone behind him, finishing an explanation about some FA rule or other.

'Chris! What's all this about?' he asked as soon as he realised who he was opening the door to. He started to look even more worried. 'This isn't bad news, is it?'

'Yes and no,' replied Chris.

Priest stood on the steps of the clubhouse, watching the action going on all over the training ground. There were close to 300 young players showing off their skills in front of him, drilled by the United coaching staff. Watching them was an even larger group of parents, supporters and other observers, including the local press. It was the biggest audience the trials had ever attracted, but then Priest knew that there had never been a year as important as this one.

The trial attracted youngsters from all over the country. Throughout the year the club's scouts had approached players they liked the look of and invited them along. In some cases, the distance involved was just too much; Priest noticed that a Scottish lad he had been very keen on hadn't turned up. However, for some of these boys distance wasn't an issue. One keen father had gone as far as to move his business down from Sheffield last Christmas, just to be on-hand to give his son a chance to get into the new school.

Looking around at the visitors who had crowded into London Road, Priest realised that he could put a name to 90 per cent of them – and that was just the adults. He knew all of the 300 lads (and 25 girls) attending the trial. Almost half were currently members of the youth squad at United, looking to hold on to their places for another year. It had been a disappointing eighteen months for the existing squad and everyone knew that Priest was looking to make changes. In many ways, the lads currently on United's books were the most nervous ones there.

Of the rest, about twenty were from different teams in the District League and another 50 from other leagues around the county. Many of the remainder were local boys too, playing with school teams or small leagues. That left another 30 to 40 who had been spotted at other trials by the scouts, or who had made an impression during a game witnessed by one of the United people.

Now they were all competing for just 135 places.

The limit wasn't the club's idea, it was an FA regulation. Even though Priest knew that many of the lads here would find places at other clubs, he still felt sorry that he was going to have to disappoint so many of them.

The players all knew the score, which was why every last one of them was giving 100 per cent out on the training pitches.

Of course, the trial was just the last phase in a long examination of all the players the club had come into contact with. Hundreds – thousands – of other players had been seen all over the place by the coaches, the scouts and by others whose eye the club trusted. And it wasn't as simple as saying that the lads who did best during the trial would get a place. Priest and the other coaches were giving everyone a last chance to show what they could do, but they had seen everyone play plenty of times before.

A few names were already pencilled in on the eight squad lists. Priest had already decided, for example, that he was going to bring in Russell Jones as one of the goalkeepers, even though he had only been playing for the Colts a little while. Russell was determined, skilful and worked hard. He had a natural eye and good balance. Finding a good keeper for the Colts had been a priority for Priest a year ago, and this was the reason why.

At least one other Colts player was in with a shout too. All the coaching staff liked the look of Rory Blackstone.

As soon as he thought of Rory, Priest began searching for the Irish lad's strike partner with the Colts. It didn't take him long. Chris's fluid movement and that mop of blond hair were things he would recognise anywhere. Chris was taking part in a two-player drill, with wide players hitting over crosses for the central strikers to head towards goal. Even as he watched, one of the coaching staff rolled a ball through for Nicky Fiorentini to chase after. He went after it like a hare,

169

controlled it with one touch and sent over a scorching, flat cross to the near post. Chris had been signalled forward to meet it.

Priest chuckled to himself as the ball rasped into the back of the net. He'd seen that combination a few times in the last two years.

'Stephens is pretty good, isn't he?' came a voice from his side.

'Yeah, pretty good,' agreed Priest dreamily. It came to him slowly who he was talking to. He turned to face the bearded man at his side, who was watching the frantic activity in front of them with keen interest.

'How do you –?' Priest began, but the answer to his question came into his mind before he needed to finish it. 'Of course, I forgot; you met Chris and his mate Nicky at Star Park the other day.'

'An interesting boy,' the other man said.

Priest turned back to the front. 'You can say that again,' he sighed.

They both watched for a few minutes in silence. Nicky delivered another pin-point cross for a young lad with spiky blond hair, who climbed and directed the ball down well, though without a lot of power. Chris's next effort, supplied by Simon Giles, one of the existing members of the youth squad, rattled off the bar. It seemed to Priest that Chris hadn't taken off very well, as if he was being cautious when he jumped.

Was he still carrying the injury? It didn't seem likely that it would have affected him this long, but Priest noticed the heavy, padded sleeve Chris was wearing under his shirt and realised that something was still wrong.

'What was he after when he came to see you earlier?' the other man asked.

Priest laughed softly. 'He says he's found something out about an ex-player for United, a guy who played back before the First World War. I didn't get all of it, but apparently Chris read a journal this guy wrote and has a replica United shirt with the old colours . . . it's all very confusing.'

He turned round to face the other man, smiling as various memories came flooding back into his mind. It had been a long eighteen months since he had first heard the name Chris

Stephens. 'Actually, Richard, you don't have to be around Chris very long to get confused. He attracts all kinds of stuff, like an adventure magnet. He can't help himself.'

Richard Branson found himself smiling as well. He'd obviously come to the same conclusion himself. In just a few seconds outside his office, Dennis Lively had been transformed from an intelligent businessman into a frothing football fan, just because Chris had some project to do with a former player.

'Will he make the squad, do you think?' he asked.

'I'm not sure,' said Priest. Although he was pretty sure that Chris was just the sort of player United needed, not all of the other coaches agreed. It would be his final decision, but he wanted everyone to be in agreement if possible.

There was a simple choice to be made. There was room for three strikers in the squad based on Chris's age group. The best of the bunch were Rory Blackstone, Alan Swain, Stewart (the spiky blond), a rough and ready target man from Leeds called Paul Massey and Chris. Three would make it; two would not. Up until now, the youth team had had Swain in partnership with Stewart, with a third boy named Richardson in reserve. They'd done pretty well as a pairing. It would take a top-rate performance from Chris (or one of the others) to shake them loose.

Chris hadn't managed to impress too many people the year before. Although there had been glowing reports of his progress with the Colts, he still had to show himself to be the right choice.

As of now, that wasn't happening.

Chris slumped wearily to the ground, trying to get his wind back. The morning session was over. It had not gone well.

He tugged impatiently at the sleeve Dr Loenikov had given him. It was starting to itch where he was sweating underneath, and he felt sure it was affecting him, weighing heavily on his arm like that. Chris was normally a more than decent header of the ball; today he had been badly off-target.

'How do you feel?' asked Nicky, looking suspiciously bright.

'Still sore. I'm not sure this thing is helping.'

Nicky's expression changed at once to concern for his

friend. 'I meant how do you feel about how it's been going. I didn't know your arm was still causing you trouble.'

Chris sighed deeply and started unlacing his boots. 'I think the answer would have been almost the same. It feels like it's been going lousy – and I'm not sure this thing is helping.'

Nicky didn't say anything, but Chris could tell he'd hoped Chris's news would have been better than that. It was obvious Nicky had had a fine morning.

'How's it going from your end?' he asked, which meant the subject could be changed with little effort.

Nicky was immediately beaming from ear to ear. 'I think I've cracked it this year! One of the coaches was really impressed with the commitment I showed.' He paused for a moment, as if wondering if that sounded a little too modest. 'I think they already know I'm the best ball-player here.'

'No doubt about it,' said Chris genuinely. 'Hardly worth their while making you take part in the six-a-sides after lunch.'

Nicky wasn't very skilful when it came to spotting any sarcasm in Chris's voice. He grinned sheepishly and lowered his eyes. 'I don't think it's as easy as that, Chris! Besides, don't you want me to help you get through as well?'

On another occasion, Chris might have been offended by Nicky's blatant over-confidence, but today he was feeling pretty calm about the way things were going.

'I get the impression I might have shot my bolt,' he confessed. 'Have you seen much of how the other strikers in our group are doing?'

Nicky looked around, making sure no-one he was about to name was in earshot.

'Your mate Rory seemed to be doing OK. He's not the fastest thing on two legs, but he looked sharp this morning. I think he's in with a chance.'

'Have you seen anything of Alan Swain?' Chris asked.

'Not a lot. He didn't look that good to me. I thought he was supposed to be two-footed? Every shot he took was off his right peg. And he looks very slow. Even on today's showing, they'd have to pick you rather than him. And you've got all this other stuff on your back.'

'Alan has his problems too,' Chris reminded him. 'You wouldn't want a dad like his.'

Nicky uttered a grunt of displeasure. 'If he didn't like the way things were turning out, he shouldn't have come. I notice his old man hasn't shown.'

Chris really didn't want to get into the whole Frank Swain business again. 'What about the others?'

It took Nicky a moment to realise they were talking football again. 'Forget Stewart. He's OK in the air, but he's useless with his feet. Rory would be a better target man any day. Or that lad from Leeds. That's about it in our age group. You're easily better than any of them, really.'

That 'really' on the end said it all. Even Nicky could see that Chris wasn't performing on the day.

At one end of the strip of grass they were sitting on, a group of caterers were beginning to serve lunch. At the other, the coaches were getting ready for the afternoon six-a-sides. Chris knew which hunger he needed to deal with first. The sooner they got back out there again, the better.

Each year group was going to play in ten-minute periods, swapping players around after each break and then starting again. Players would change ends, even change sides, and would be rotated in and out so that the coaches could see them in different positions with different partners.

'I've got to show them what I can do,' Chris muttered to himself.

He turned to Nicky again, to share an idea with him, but Fiorentini was already on his way to lunch. Naturally, he avoided the fare served up by the caterers and went to see what his mother had packed in the umpteen cool-bags weighing down the trunk of the Fiorentini car.

Actually, Chris thought, some of Mrs Fiorentini's pasta would go down just right about now. He wondered if she had prepared enough for one more. Then he scolded himself for asking such a daft question and walked over to join his team mate.

Twenty

Chris latched on to a through ball from Nicky that had split two defenders and left the goalkeeper in two minds about whether to come off his line. Finishing off a chance like that was just about the easiest thing he'd ever done, but he made sure he placed the ball perfectly, bending it around the stranded goal-minder into the far corner.

'Pick that out!' yelled Nicky as he ran over to congratulate his partner.

They trotted back to their own half, noticing that the coaches were about to blow time on the last period of the six-a-sides. There wasn't even time to restart the game before the whistles started to blow.

'That clinches it!' yelled Nicky, swatting at the air with his fist. 'Goodbye Spirebrook, hello Oldcester United!'

He caught Chris looking across at him in a scolding manner and made a face that was half-apology/half-confident smirk. 'I know, I know . . . we've still got two terms at the old dump first.'

'There's also the small matter of getting selected,' Chris reminded him.

Nicky wasn't thinking about that at all and, in fairness, Chris knew he didn't have to. Nicky had played brilliantly all day. The club would have to be mad not to take him after the show he'd put on.

He could see Nicky was about to say something like that himself, so he quickly nudged his team mate into shaking a few hands and offering 'well-dones' to the other players in their group.

The coaches were handing out bottles of drink and herding the tired players back towards the clubhouse. Chris noticed a few winks and nods being offered, as some of them let certain players know they'd done well. 'The Terminator' put his arm round Nicky's shoulders, which seemed to suggest that Nicky's confidence was not misplaced.

Slowly, the young players gathered together, seeking out their closest friends and team mates. Chris managed to track down Zak and the other members of the Colts team. Zak had been as good as told he'd made it – he'd be in the year group above the one Chris and Nicky were aiming for. Russell was completely confused by the whole thing; Rory looked a little out of shape. Stamp had managed to get into an argument with another player that had almost come to blows, which he was sure had ruined his chances.

'What about you, Chris?' asked Zak.

'I had a better afternoon,' Chris replied. 'This stupid sleeve is getting on my nerves though.'

'Why don't you take it off?' asked Zak, which seemed a fair question.

'Because it's protecting his arm, stupid!' scoffed Nicky. 'Blimey, how did you get to be the Colts' captain?'

Chris tried a more tactful approach. 'I took a couple of knocks earlier. It's just as well I wore it.'

Nicky's eyes suddenly glazed over as if he was staring into the distance. 'Yeah, I meant to ask about that. You got some problem with Joe Maguire?' Maguire was a ball-winner in midfield, a member of the existing United squad. Chris didn't really know him at all. 'He gave you a couple of whacks early on, didn't he?'

Chris realised that Nicky wasn't just staring aimlessly off into the distance, he was focused on Maguire's sandy-coloured hair, poking out above a small knot of United youth team players some short distance to their left. 'That kid with the earring and the dark hair, the one beside Maguire; he banged into you a few times as well.'

Chris remembered only too well. The dark-haired lad was called Foster and he'd collided with Chris going up for a high ball. About a minute later he'd almost succeeded in tripping Chris in an off-the-ball tackle. Maguire, too, had been pulling and pushing at him whenever he had been on the opposite side.

'What are you suggesting, Nicky?' asked Chris.

'Nothing!' insisted Nicky, in a fake show of innocence. 'But did you notice how they didn't give Alan Swain anything like so rough a ride? He scored three goals my gran could have made! And Maguire and Foster didn't try any of that rough stuff with Rory, either . . .'

'I'd have broken their noses,' muttered Rory. It sounded all the more effective as a threat for being spoken with his soft Irish accent, although Chris knew that there wasn't a player there less likely to get involved in a fight than his Colts' team mate.

'You think they're trying to get Chris injured again?' gasped Zak.

Nicky just shrugged.

'It wouldn't have hurt if Swain had had some of the same treatment,' muttered Stamp with a dark rumble in his voice.

'Hang on,' said Chris. 'You don't know that something is going on. And even if those two apes are trying to get heavy, it doesn't mean Alan Swain is involved. Look, it's not like he's hanging round with them – he's over by that other group.'

No-one bothered to give Swain much more than a brief glance. Nicky's theory had struck a chord with all of them, and they were much more interested in how they were going to sort the situation out.

'Nicky . . .' pleaded Chris, but he could tell that events were overtaking him fast.

Fortunately, a welcome distraction arrived before anyone could actually get to their feet and go over to sort Maguire and Foster out.

'Mr Foulds,' said Nicky, beaming, instantly sweetness and light once more. 'Long time, no see.'

Foulds was the scout who had first introduced Chris and Nicky to the idea of coming to United's trial the year before. They hadn't seen much of him since, although he turned up to some of the District League games they took part in. He'd always said hello, and the boys had the idea he liked to keep an eye on how they were doing.

'Hello, Nicky,' Foulds replied wearily (and he hadn't even been talking to Nicky that long!). 'How's it going?'

'All right,' Nicky asserted, smiling with satisfaction. 'Come to tell us the good news?'

'About what?'

That took a little of the wind out of Nicky's sails. 'The trials, of course!'

'Not my job,' Foulds told him, and Chris fancied that the scout was enjoying geeing Nicky up. 'Sean Priest will let you know how things went.'

Nicky had been hoping to get a little advance inside information. He sank back, sitting with his hands splayed behind him for support, mumbling about how these things always took so long.

'Do you have a minute, Chris?' Foulds asked, beckoning for him to follow.

They stepped away from the others, walking slowly through the crowd. Chris saw his father watching them, and shrugged to show he had no idea what this was in aid of either.

'Here's how it goes,' said Foulds, getting straight to the point. 'The coaches are finishing off their discussions about who gets into next year's squads now. They have three lists.' He ticked them off on his fingers. 'The ones who have definitely made it, the ones who are going to be told to try again next year and the ones in the middle. You're on the third list.'

Chris felt a moment of intense disappointment, but it passed almost right away. Last year, they hadn't even got this close; this year, if the trials were having much of an influence, he'd blown it because of that stupid injury.

'So what does that mean?' he asked, ready for the worst.

'It means that there are a few places where the coaches can't make up their minds. Yours is one. To put it bluntly, you've not convinced everyone you have the ability to make the grade.'

Chris kept silent, listening carefully.

'A few of us have seen you all year, on or off. We know what you can do. And your record speaks for itself. The trouble is, those members of the coaching staff who have only seen you at this trial and last year's haven't seen the best of Chris Stephens. Their concern is that, on the big occasion, you don't have what it takes.'

That hurt. Chris wanted to argue, but what would be the point? He was supposed to have shown what he was capable of on the pitch.

'Do you understand what I'm saying?' asked Foulds. 'It's called commitment. This new school is going to be the biggest thing that's ever happened to this club and to the whole game in England. The continentals have had systems like this for years. Look at the young players in the Ajax team! All home grown!' His voice had grown louder with enthusiasm as he made that point, but it softened again for the next sentence. 'The lads who get asked to take part in this new scheme have got to be ready to give everything they have to the school and the club. It means being ready to dig deep; to work even harder for the big prize.'

He paused, gathering his thoughts. 'Think of it this way. Think of some of the great Cup upsets you've seen over the years. Remember York City doing Manchester United? Or Sutton beating Coventry? You look at the two teams on paper, and its a walk-over for the bigger club. So what happens?

'It's simple. On the day, those giant killers wanted it more than the big club. They raised their game for the occasion. If you want to be a part of this club – if you want it as much as I think you do – you've got to dig deep, right now.'

'Now?' asked Chris. 'Why now?'

'Because they're going to invite the boys on that third list to take part in one last game. One last chance to show what they can do. It's between you and Alan Swain who gets to be part of the squad next year.'

'So we'll be on different teams?'

'No . . .' replied Foulds. 'You'll be on the same team.'

That idea took a bit of getting used to. While Chris pondered, Foulds finished off with one last piece of advice.

'You've already convinced Sean and I that you can do it Chris. Just get out there and show the others . . .'

Chris was still thinking, still trying to get his brain awake enough to face one last trial when a voice popped up from the rear.

'Hang on a minute!'

Chris and Ray Foulds turned around slowly. They didn'

need to look to see whose familiar, piercing voice it was, but neither of them could quite believe it. When they faced Nicky, they realised he was pretty hot under the collar.

'Nicky . . .'

Fiorentini paid Chris no attention at all, but steamed on to make his point. 'If Sean Priest thinks Chris is good enough, and he's the boss, why isn't that it? Why does Chris have to prove himself to anyone else?'

'That's not how it works,' sighed Foulds, who was as used to Nicky's outbursts as anyone. 'Or, at least, it's not how Sean works. He wants everyone around him to believe in the club, the school and the players. He doesn't want anyone who hasn't earned his place clean and clear.'

'But Chris has earned his place!' Nicky insisted. 'He's a much better player than Alan Swain. Listen, you don't know what's been going on. Chris has been injured!'

'That's been taken into account,' Foulds began.

Nicky cut him off just after the 'been'. 'No, I mean today! Swain's dad had a word with a couple of the other boys; told them Chris was carrying an injury to his arm! They've been clattering into Chris all day!'

That was news to Foulds, who raised an eyebrow as he digested the news.

'How can . . .'

'Oh, I can prove it all right. Me and Stamp have been beating it out of Joe Maguire.'

'Nicky!' cried Chris, utterly amazed.

Nicky managed to look quite hurt at Chris's obvious criticism. Then a small smile crept over his face. 'Oh, all right, so maybe Stamp did the beating and I just listened.' He slowly realised that this wasn't the point as far as Chris was concerned. 'Look, Stamp's failed the trial, so it doesn't matter anyway.' He waited to see if Chris felt any better about that, but realised that he still hadn't found the right words to reassure his team mate. 'OK, OK, it was just a few threats. And one slap. No-one noticed; honest!'

Chris sighed. As always, Nicky had gone right to the heart of the problem as soon as Chris's back was turned, and run over it in studded DMs. He was as subtle as a brieze block.

'Nicky, you just can't . . .' he began. Words failed him. Nicky was looking at him with the words 'I did it for you!' safely stashed away in his brain. He didn't need to say them; they both knew what the score was.

'I don't quite understand what this is all about,' said Foulds.

'OK,' said Nicky, always prepared to spell the facts out to anyone less aware of what was going on than he was (which he didn't get to do very often). Naturally, the explanation had to be counted out on his fingers. 'One, Chris had a run-in with Alan's dad yesterday; two, Swain knew Chris had hurt his arm – and he tried to make it worse by throwing him out of the house. Three, he slipped the Braindead Brothers a tenner each to nobble Chris during the trial. It was always going to come down to either Chris or Alan today, so he tried to make sure that Alan won.'

Nicky grinned broadly, pleased with his own summing up of the case. Foulds was still thinking.

'Who else knows about this?' he asked.

'No-one yet, but I think we have to tell Sean right away.'

'What was this run-in with Swain all about, though?' asked Foulds. Chris wondered how many fingers Nicky would need to explain that. At the same moment, he decided he didn't want to find out.

'Enough, Nicky!' he snapped, as Nicky's mouth opened.

'Yes, but –'

'No!' Chris's voice was as hard and firm as ice. Nicky flinched and fell silent. 'I've told Sean everything he needs to know today about the whole business,' he continued. He knew that Nicky would understand what that meant, even if they were leaving Foulds looking more and more bemused. 'Whatever his dad may or may not have done, it isn't down to Alan. We still have to sort out which of us belongs in the squad.'

'Yes, but –'

'Can it, Nicky!' Chris insisted. 'I mean that!'

And, to his amazement, Nicky fell silent.

Chris turned his attention to Ray Foulds. 'I can't stop you telling Sean what you've just heard, but leave it until after this last game, OK?'

Foulds nodded. 'I admire you, Chris. Wanting to give Alan a fair crack of the whip like this.'

'It's not about Alan,' Chris replied instantly. 'It's about me.'

And, in a strange roundabout kind of way, about another guy who was cheated out of his place on the team by a false accusation, 80 years before . . .

'Listen up, all of you!'

Sean's voice carried across the hushed group in front of him, loud and clear. There was no way he had actually needed to tell anyone to listen to him. Everyone was completely focused on what he had to say.

'Thanks to all of you for coming today and working so hard. We've seen a lot of very talented players. During the day, we've firmed up our impressions about who we want to see in the squad next year. However, there are still a few loose ends we want to clear up. So, while we go off and talk some more, we'd like a few of you to play one last game on the full pitch, eleven-a-side, twenty minutes each way. We've drawn up two teams of about equal strength. If you're in one of those teams, we'd like you to dig deep and give us one last effort.

'I ought to point out,' he said quickly as whispers started to flow round the group, 'that if you're on this list I'm about to read out, it doesn't mean you're in the squad or out. Nor does it mean anything if you're *not* on this list. We'll tell all of you who we want to sign on after this last match is over.'

He lifted up the clipboard in his hand as if he was about to read from it right away. Then he looked around at the eager faces below him and paused.

'Before I read out the two teams,' he said, 'I want to tell you a short story I heard today. Since I heard it, I've been thinking a lot about what it means to pull on this shirt –' He indicated the brand new United shirt he was wearing '– or any of its predecessors. Apparently, so the story goes, there was this lad, who was born and raised in the shadow of the old Star Park ground. He grew up to be a decent footballer. When he was about fifteen, he got the chance to fulfil a dream that had been growing up inside him since he first started to play football in the street. He got the chance to play for United.

'Then, on what should have been the proudest day of his

life, he was cheated of that chance. He didn't get to pull on a United shirt and run out on to the field in front of thousands of fans, all chanting his name and wishing they were him. And he didn't get another chance, either. There was a war, and he went off to fight for his country. And like millions of others, he never came back.

'The only reason we know about this guy is because there was a book, a small notebook he wrote in the year or so before he died. Sadly, the book was destroyed, but someone else had read it by then; someone who was also mad keen to wear a United shirt. He told me the story of this guy, and now I'm telling it to you.'

He paused, taking a long look around at the half-circle of faces looking back at him. No-one was so much as breathing.

'Why am I telling you this? Because you all have a chance still to realise that dream, if you want it badly enough. Whatever happens today, you still have that chance. This guy, he only had one shot at it, and then it was gone.' Sean laughed, but there was sadness in his voice. 'I think if that had happened to me, I would have been so ticked off I'd have bust out of heaven and come back here to try and play again.'

There was a small ripple of laughter. The Terminator mentioned that Priest would probably have made sure that heaven had a youth team before he left, and the laughter continued.

'The guy's name was William Murdoch. Remember that name. Remember what he lost, and what you've got. A chance. A dream. If you remember well enough, and work for it, then one day you'll pull on a shirt like this — and it'll be a real one.'

Even though he knew the story better than anyone, Chris had a lump in his throat at the end of that speech. Some of the other lads appeared almost stunned by what they had heard. At his side, Chris heard Nicky whisper 'Yeah!' Priest had fired up every last one of them.

Priest cleared his throat and lifted the clipboard, preparing to read out the names.

'Actually, Sean, do you mind if I interrupt?'

Chris looked back to the front. Looking just a little out of place, and stepping forward awkwardly from the background,

Richard Branson was walking forward, carrying a kit bag. As he got level with Priest, he reached inside.

'The same person who told us the story about William Murdoch this morning gave us this – it's a copy of the kind of shirt they used to wear back then, or so I'm told. The other day, at Sean's benefit game, I showed you the shirt we were planning to use next season, the one Sean is wearing now. I've been looking at it all day, since I heard the story, and I realised the designers have made a mistake. They thought stripes would make it difficult to read the sponsors' logo. I don't think it matters. So, I've made an executive decision. As of next season, Virgin Cola's name will be on this shirt instead . . .'

He held up the jersey from Chris's bag. There was a moment when no-one said anything, when they just looked and thought. Then about 100 of the 300 players (plus quite a few adults) pumped their fists and yelled 'Yes!'

Chris had yelled louder than any of them. 'I know it's stupid,' he told Nicky, 'but United without stripes just wouldn't have been right.'

'Yeah,' sighed Nicky. 'I know.'

It took quite a few minutes for the fuss to die down. By that time Richard Branson had put the shirt back in the bag and stepped away into the background. Meanwhile, looking around him furtively, Priest had pulled the new jersey off over his head, revealing that he had been wearing last season's strip underneath all along.

He held up his hand to try and restore order. The clipboard was in his hand once more, raised ready for him to read the names on it.

'Uh – Sean?'

Priest appeared quite frustrated for a moment, but slowly lifted his eyes from the clipboard to see who had created this latest interruption (it had escaped his mind that he had stopped himself reading the list the first time).

'Alan?'

Chris lifted his head above the crowd at the mention of that name, catching a glimpse of Alan Swain slowly standing up. Unfortunately, everyone else was craning their necks or climbing to their knees to get a better view, so he lost sight of Swain almost as quickly as he had spotted him. Nicky – who lacked a few inches on Chris anyway – was already on his feet. Chris decided to follow his lead.

Alan Swain was the centre of everyone's attention.

'That story you just told us. I know a bit more about it . . . I mean. I know something . . .' his voice trailed off.

Priest thought about telling Alan that he'd be pleased to hear the rest of the tale later, but that they had finished with the inspirational speeches for now, and that it was time to get on with the football. However, there was something so miserable and guilty about Alan's expression that he decided it had better come out now. It didn't appear to be something Alan could hold inside any longer.

'What do you mean?' he asked.

It took Alan a moment to get going. He was clearly struggling with something inside.

'You said about there being a book. The book William Murdoch wrote about his life. You said it had been destroyed.'

Priest nodded, wondering where this was leading. A short distance away, Chris was having the same thoughts.

'Uh –' Alan began, his voice trembling. 'Apart from all the football stuff, there's some other stuff in the book; stuff my father didn't want people to know.' Chris felt his stomach turn. He knew what Alan was about to do; he could tell it by the way his voice was turning in on itself, and the way he was struggling to find any other word in his head other than 'stuff'.

Suddenly, the confession sprung out, as if it had been caged inside and at last saw a way to escape.

'My dad burned the book.'

Chris's heart missed a beat. It wasn't that what he was hearing was news in any way, but he had been clutching on to a small hope that maybe Swain wouldn't have carried out his threat. That hope was gone now.

'I see . . .' Priest was saying, even if he didn't.

'My dad's been saying for ages that he's writing a book himself. He's borrowed pictures and other stuff from all kinds of people – including the club and lots of the people here . . . It was supposed to be a big history of the club. It was going to tell the whole story.'

Alan was sounding a bit more together, as if having started

to reveal the truth, it was coming out cleanly now, almost without his help.

'That was a lie. He never intended to write anything. He's been stealing anything about the club he could lay his hands on. There are boxes and boxes of it on the floor of every room in the house.' He took a moment to gather his thoughts; everyone else took the same moment to let the information sink in. Most of them knew about Swain and his book; some of them may even have suspected that it would never be written. This, though, was something else.

'It's worse than that. My grandad was a thief too. He started the whole thing off. Back in the 1920s, he started a fire which destroyed the old Star Park, the first one, over by the station. No-one ever knew. And no-one could have guessed that before he started the fire, he stole a whole load of stuff from the office. Some silver, a few books, and loads of old photos. Some of you know he was a player back then. When United said they were letting him go, he couldn't accept it. So he took everything he could lay his hands on from the years he'd been playing. It's been hidden in our house ever since.'

'I knew it!' cried Chris, and it caught him by surprise when he realised that he'd said it loud enough for Priest, Alan Swain and about 500 other people to hear.

The silence afterwards was like a vacuum. Some of the bemused audience who had listened to the unfolding drama were looking at Chris. Others were looking at Alan. This was better than telly.

'I'm really sorry, Chris,' Alan began.

At which point a fourth individual joined in the fun.

'Yeah, right! I suppose you're really sorry about the way your father tried to have Chris crocked so that you'd get back into the squad?'

Chris groaned. Trust Nicky to up the stakes even further.

'I never –' Alan began.

Nicky laughed mockingly, and prepared to launch into a further set of accusations or proofs. Others might have been feeling a little awkward, standing up in front of a crowd, but Fiorentini DNA was missing the embarrassment gene.

'Nicky! Give up!' snarled Chris, in the best warning whisper he could manage. He didn't manage to silence his mate, but

Nicky was distracted enough that he turned away from Alan, who used that moment to get his head back together.

'I know all that,' he said. 'That's why I had to say all this now, before the trials were over. I had to let you all know . . . especially you, Chris . . .'

He bent down, picking up his jacket, and reached into one of the pockets. When he stood up again, he was holding a charred notebook. Chris recognised it at once.

'I rescued the book, as quickly as I could. I'm afraid some of it got burned . . . all the stuff at the back . . .'

'The bits I copied!' Chris shouted. That meant the story could be saved. William's story *would* be remembered properly.

'Now that I've told you about the stuff my father stole,' Alan was continuing, speaking directly to Priest, 'you can get all that back too.' He turned to face Chris. 'There's even the original of that team photo, the one with William Murdoch in.'

Chris was almost ready to leap into the air. It had all come good at last.

'Which just leaves one last thing,' said Alan, now facing Priest once more. 'Seeing what my dad's been up to, I don't see how I can stay in the squad. So, whatever you've decided, I've made up my mind to leave the team.'

Gasps and whispers ran around the audience (which was the only way Chris could think of them now). A few of them were utterly confused, but they'd all understood that last sentence clearly. At the front, Priest was looking down at the clipboard, and the two names in the blue team, one under the other. Stephens and Swain. It appeared the decision between them had been made.

'Oh no you don't!' called Chris.

He stepped forward to the front, advancing towards where Swain was standing, surrounded by some of the other members of the existing squad. 'This last game, it's partly to decide whether you or I get a place in the squad. You can't back down now.'

That really threw Swain out of his stride. 'But I thought . . .' he said.

'Don't think. Play. Didn't you hear what Sean said earlier? You can't just walk away from this.'

'But –'

'Are you listening to me? All your life you've played to please your father. Well, he's finished now. I expect he'll get arrested or something. You've got all that to deal with, starting tomorrow.

'But right now, you've got a chance to play for yourself. To show yourself that you really are better than your old man, or his old man. This is your chance to show that you *deserve* to wear a United shirt.'

Alan's eyes were open so wide Chris was afraid they'd snap in the corners. Swain clearly didn't understand what was going on.

'But surely you want my place . . .'

'Well of course I do!' snapped Chris. 'I'm not giving it to you, you dope. Don't you get it? I'm going to show my best out there, and I want you to do the same. That way, when I beat you, it will be fair and square. I'll have won my place, not had it given to me.'

Alan continued to gape at him as if he would never be able to start a sentence again that didn't have the word 'but' as the first word. Chris looked at Sean, who shrugged to prove that he didn't understand it either, but that he was prepared to go along with anything that would settle the issue. Everyone else was waiting for Alan Swain.

'OK . . .' Alan said at last.

'Good,' said Chris, grinning. 'Let's do it.'

Twenty-one

———————— ⚽ ————————

It would have been too much to have expected that last game to be very wonderful. The boys were all tired, and they had just been on an amazing rollercoaster ride, following the path Chris, Alan and Nicky had led them on.

On the other hand, every one of them knew that this was the last opportunity they would have at the trials to snatch one of the undecided places.

It was hard; it was competitive. Some of the players really did dig deeper than they had ever done before, pulling out gutsy, committed performances that finally convinced the watching coaches that they had the right stuff.

No-one was more pumped up than Chris. After taking a bruising tackle in the first minute, he had walked to the touchline and pointedly removed the protective sleeve in front of Foster and Maguire. Dr Loenikov hid his eyes behind his hand, but soon he was applauding the decision along with everyone else.

Without that weight on his arm, Chris felt better balanced. The red team's defenders didn't get within a mile of him from then on.

Swain started slowly, as if all his energy had gone out of him. However, when Chris knocked on a through ball after ten minutes, Alan's instincts took over and he raced in on goal. The keeper pulled off a miraculous save to deny the opening score.

It took Chris those first ten minutes to realise that the red team seemed to be older, taller and bigger than the blues. He suspected that was Sean's way of making it harder. Normally, he fancied his chances in the air against any defence, but he quickly rounded up the midfield players while the ball was out of play and told them to hit passes to feet.

'Put the ball behind them. They don't look to have a lot of speed, especially down their left. Quick passes, and lots of running off the ball – that'll do it for us.'

It took less than a minute for the new plan to get tried out. Chris sprinted sideways across the pitch as one of the players he had just spoken to picked up the ball from defence, bringing it out wide. Timing the moment perfectly, Chris turned sharply and went upfield beyond his marker just as the ball was played in from the touchline. One of the centre backs moved across to meet him, expecting Chris to collect the ball, but Chris just stepped over the rolling ball, ran round him and picked it up on the other side. He was in space, ten metres from the corner of the penalty box, with the goal begging.

Which was when he noticed that Alan was in an even better position, dead centre. He didn't think, he just hit the pass square. Alan thrashed it into the net.

As they changed ends at half-time, he saw Nicky screwing his finger against the side of his head as if he thought Chris had gone mad.

The goal lifted Alan's mood, and he played a blinding second half. At first he pushed up, sucking in the three-man back row the reds were using, collecting passes from the midfielders and laying off returns at a pace the defenders couldn't live with. Just when they'd got used to that, he took one pass, spun 180 degrees on the spot, and hit a dipping shot that the keeper palmed over the bar.

For the last ten minutes he played deeper, dragging the confused defenders along with him and leaving acres of space for the other members of the blue team to run into. His passes were direct and unfancy, hitting the right man in the right place at the right speed. The blues were all over their bigger opponents. Their goalkeeper collected two wild clearances and a back pass during the whole second half.

Alan's performance deserved to be recognised. It was, though, only the second best performance on the field.

In that first phase, when Alan was acting as a target man, Chris dropped into the style he used with the Colts, playing wider. He ran the full back ragged. Both with the ball and without it, Chris was moving fluently, finding space, creating havoc.

When he ran with the ball, it was just like William was there, showing him how to stay balanced, how to keep his control tight. The defenders never even saw a sniff of a chance to make a tackle.

When Alan dropped back, Chris took advantage to move inside and take the central role he normally played in at school. The defence had about had enough by then. Chris even found himself winning clean headers.

The blues deserved a second goal, but the red keeper was making sure that the coaches wouldn't be able to ignore him. One point-blank drive from Swain threatened to knock his head off, but he caught the ball in front of his face and rolled it out to the full back as if it had been a balloon.

The Terminator was about ready to call time. Chris saw the coach look at his watch as he dashed over the halfway line again. This was the last chance.

There was no obvious channel up the right or the middle, so Chris angled across to the other side. Suddenly, there was space. He lifted his arm and called, looking back to see where the ball was.

It was on its way. Swain had driven a low, skidding pass through a tiny gap. It was perfectly weighted for Chris to pick up. The only problem was that it had gone a little wide.

Sensibly, Chris should have run on to it, taken it wide and then held it up to wait for the others to come up in support. But he could feel how close The Terminator was to calling time. Instinctively, he pounced on the ball.

He was twenty metres out, shooting off his left foot, and side on to goal. The red keeper was perfectly placed, on the edge of the six-metre box, narrowing the angle. It should never have been a chance, never mind a goal.

The keeper was still standing in the same spot when the ball hit the back of the net. It had looped, swerved and flashed past him like a missile. The loud cheer that went up a second later was like a sonic boom.

'You OK?' asked Chris.

Swain nodded. He was relieved to see that even Nicky was smiling now.

'No problem,' he said, continuing to pack his kit into his bag. 'You know what you're going to do?'

He nodded. 'I'm going to go home and tell my dad that the game's up. I'm sure he'll realise the best thing to do is to hand all the stuff back without any fuss.'

Chris hoped that was true. However, he was worried about the other possibilities. 'But what if . . .'

'My dad gets arrested and goes to prison? Sean says he doesn't think it'll come to that, if everything is given back. But even if it does, we'll manage. I have an aunt who lives nearby; I could stay with her. And then . . .'

'And then?' asked Chris.

'And then I'm going to come back next year and get my place back.'

Chris smiled. He would like to see Alan try.

'Listen, we ought to be getting going,' said Nicky. 'My mum wants to get home and cook a victory feast. She's already invited Zak and Rory . . . not to mention Sean Priest and half the coaches.' He glanced down at the ground for a moment, then flicked back his hair and looked at Swain. 'You want to come?'

Chris watched him think it over, but knew what the answer would be.

'Nah . . . thanks, but I think I'd better just get home.'

Nicky stuck out his hand and Alan shook it. Then Swain did the same with Chris.

'Good luck,' said Chris.

'And you,' said Alan. 'Look after that shirt for me.'

'Yeah . . .' laughed Chris. 'Hey, you might want to give the Colts a ring. They'll need a good striker now . . .'

'No change there then,' said Nicky.

There was plenty more they could have said, but it would keep. Chris led Nicky away. Alan watched them go, joining up with Chris's father, a varied collection of other players and guests, and a long line of black-haired people who seemed to be able to all talk and listen at once. They were almost having to carry Rory Blackstone out, who kept muttering 'they picked me, they picked *me*' as he was carted away.

The book was in Priest's safe-keeping. It was time to go home and face the music.

A few people muttered goodbyes as he set off towards the exit. He didn't look back. He was determined that this wasn't going to be the last time he went through these gates. As he stepped out on to the street, one last voice added a comment that made him look up.

'You played well today.'

He didn't recognise the man leaning against the gate post. He was tall, with extremely short black hair and brilliant blue eyes. His skin was very pale. He wore a ratty old coat over dull browny-green trousers and a white shirt. He rubbed a smooth hand over the stubble on his chin, waiting for Alan to say something.

'Not good enough, though,' Alan replied.

'I don't know,' the man replied. 'Maybe it just wasn't your day.'

Alan shrugged. He felt he'd given it his best shot, but Stephens was better, there was no denying that.

'Maybe. Or maybe I just need to do some more work on my game. Chris Stephens – did you see him, he was the other lad up front with me in that last game . . .'

'I know Chris,' the man replied.

'Yeah, well, the way he ran with the ball was something else. I've watched him before, and I didn't know he could dribble like that. Someone's been coaching him.' Alan remembered watching Chris slip through tackles as if he was a ghost. It had been unbelievable.

'You could be right,' said the dark-haired man, with an odd smile.

'And that shot at the end . . .'

'I doubt if anyone taught him that,' the man agreed, and he was laughing now.

Alan smiled as well. He felt OK, talking like this. He wasn't jealous or anything. In fact, he felt quite peaceful.

'Listen,' the man said. 'If you meant what you said to Chris, about coming back next year, I'd like to help. I used to play a bit, and I'm sure there are some tricks I could show you.'

'Really?'

The man's eyes flickered with a strong, insistent power.

'Sure,' he said. 'I'd like nothing better.'

'OK,' said Alan. 'You're on. I'd be glad of the help ... uh ... I'm sorry, I don't know your name.'

The man was smiling, obviously glad that his offer had been accepted. Alan got the impression that this would mean a lot to him. He stepped forward, and put his arm on Alan's shoulder.

'You can call me William ...' he said.